Sherlock Holmes
and the
Round Table Adventure

By

Joseph W. Svec III

&

Lidia B. Svec

Paperback ISBN 978-1-78092-686-5
ePub ISBN 978-1-78092-687-2
PDF ISBN 978-1-78092-688-9

Published in the UK by MX Publishing
335 Princess Park Manor, Royal Drive,
London, N11 3GX
www.mxpublishing.co.uk

Cover design by Brian Belanger.
Chapter header images licensed from Clipart.com, except Chapter 3, image by Dr. Leedjia Svec. PhD

The author may be contacted via the webpage www.pixymuse.com

Acknowledgements:

We would like to acknowledge and thank Linda Hein and Beth Barnard for their time and outstanding effort in reviewing this book and providing comments. It is greatly appreciated.

Dedication

This book is dedicated to our children, Joseph W. Svec IV, and Dr. Leedjia Ann Svec. May your adventures be full of happiness and enchantment.

Sherlock Holmes

and the

Round Table Adventure

Table of Contents:

A Note to Readers:

The following story, *Sherlock Holmes and the Round Table Adventure*, which I refer to as book three of the Sherlock Holmes and the Missing Authors Trilogy, is one of the most odd and unusual Sherlock Holmes adventures ever written by his trusted friend and biographer, Dr. John Watson. They have shared many an adventure together over the years, and I would say Sherlock Holmes' fame is due in equal parts to Sherlock's uncanny skills in logic, perception and deduction, and Dr. Watson's outstanding skill as a scribe in collecting and recording their adventures. This manuscript was discovered at the same time as the first two books of the trilogy, and the reader may notice that it seems to contradict much of what Sherlock Holmes many times had previously stated about the absolute impossibility of magic, yet I assure you that it is presented here word-for-word just as Dr. Watson had recorded it so many years ago.

As in the previous two manuscripts, *Sherlock Holmes and the "Adventure of the Grinning Cat,"* (Book One) and *"Sherlock Holmes in the Nautilus Adventure,"* (Book Two of the Missing Authors Trilogy), Dr. Watson had requested that this story not be published until seventy five years after his passing. Again, as this document was lost for many years and has been just recently rediscovered, the requested amount of time has more than passed, so this story may be published, and presented for your consideration.

Be prepared for a very odd, yet thoroughly enchanting and magical adventure.

Prologue

Memorandum:

To: Whom it may Concern

From: Dr. John Watson M.D.

Subject: *Sherlock Holmes and the Round Table Adventure*

Date: February, 1898

I stand (figuratively speaking that is) before you, the reader, with yet another incredible tale of Sherlock Holmes and a missing author. This is the third in a series of similar adventures involving vanished literary leviathans happening in such quick succession that I am still overwhelmed by the entire experience. The first two cases involved Sherlock Holmes, searching for Lewis Carroll and Jules Verne respectively, with famous characters coming to life right from the pages of their novels and appearing in our lodgings at 221-B Baker Street. From that point, the tales grew more strange and unusual as they unfolded.

This final tale is without question the oddest of the trilogy, yet the outcome is also without question, the most satisfying. Yes, it is true that history itself was slightly altered as a result of this adventure, but in reality, Sherlock actually helped to bring about events that had already taken place. They had already happened and had been recorded, so our little foray into the past was simply the catalyst that brought them to fruition.

And without question, this is also a love story. It chronicles Sherlock's journey to meet an ethereal musical pixy whom he had previously encountered twice before in our last two adventures. He was utterly mesmerized and captivated by her hauntingly magnificent music, and he simply could not rest until he found her. Her enchanting song would not be denied.

That being said, for the sake of Sherlock's reputation as a consulting detective and his standing with Scotland Yard, and my own practice as a doctor, I must still request that this manuscript not be published until seventy-five years after my passing. Your compliance in honoring my request is appreciated.

Dr. John H. Watson M. D.

Sherlock Holmes

and the

Round Table Adventure

Chapter 1.

A Very Odd Visitor, (And a knight to remember.)

Sherlock Holmes and I looked at one another in utter disbelief. Yet another fictional character from literature was standing before us in the doorway of our lodgings at 221`B Baker Street asking for Sherlock's help in locating a missing author. We had just, days ago, concluded adventures involving the Cheshire Cat, White Rabbit, and Mad Hatter, searching for Alice of Wonderland, as well as Lewis Carroll himself, whom had both disappeared. Then Captain Nemo of the *"Nautilus"* arrived seeking to engage Sherlock in locating Jules

Verne, who was missing. Now we had a Knight of the Round Table at our door seeking Alfred Lord Tennyson? This was more than I could accept.

Our most recent adventures had left me with a terrible cold, and Sherlock in a rather forlorn and despondent state regarding an ethereal musical Pixy whom we had crossed paths with. He had heard her enchanting music on several occasions and was positively mesmerized by her. The way he described it, he was sweetly haunted by the silver toned echoes of her captivating music, and could not escape from it. Her melody was ringing in his thoughts constantly. It was akin to catching a fleeting glimpse of the most beautiful woman you have ever seen, hearing her lilting voice, as you share a brief, but unforgettable conversation with her knowing that she is that special one you have longed for eternally, but then she vanishes! The emptiness you are left with is overwhelming. There is simply nothing to fill the endless void.

Over the last several days, Sherlock, with a starry-eyed distant look had said that when he played his violin, he was somehow communicating with her, which was wonderful, but it left him longing for more. It made the ache worse. He was at a loss as to what to do. Strangely enough, when he played, I could hear echoes of her melodies playing counter point and harmony. It was beautiful and melancholy at the same time. Perhaps this odd new adventure would take Sherlock's mind off his winsome Pixy Music.

The brown haired, grey-eyed gentleman of muscular build standing before us did look convincingly like a medieval knight with well used chain mail armor over which he wore a tunic. The sword which hung from his belt also looked quite authentic. He had burst into 221-B Baker Street claiming to be Sir Percival of Camelot and was requesting Sherlock's help in locating Alfred Lord Tennyson,

England's former Poet Laureate and author of *"The Idylls of the King,"* the well known series of poems that tell the timeless tale of King Arthur and the Knights of the Round Table.

"You do know that Sir Alfred Lord Tennyson has been dead for six years," Sherlock pointed out to the armor-clad stranger standing in the doorway. "He passed away on October 6, 1892 and was buried in the Poet's Corner of Westminster Abbey near the graves of Chaucer and Robert Browning. His family was present at the time of his death. It would have been quite difficult to have contrived that, as he was one of the three most well known individuals in the country at the time. He was a personal friend of Queen Victoria, herself."

Then with a wry grin he asked, "Can I assist you in finding some other equally inaccessible person of literature, perhaps the famous poet and playwright William Shakespeare or possibly Merlin the magician?"

The stranger, however, not deterred by Sherlock's response, persisted. "Pray tell, I am not familiar with this 'shaking spear' person you mention. From his name, it sounds like he would strike fear and dread into the hearts of his readers." I thought to myself how true his statement was when it came to many students of English literature, but the knight went on speaking. "And it was Merlin the Enchanter himself who made it possible for me to be here. I know it may sound odd to you, but Alfred Lord Tennyson did not actually pass away in 1892. He just passed out of your world, or if you will, your *time period,* and into ours, and now he truly has gone missing. He has vanished! We must locate him, and Merlin made it very clear that you are the only one with the requisite skills to find him."

With a distinct note of skepticism in his voice, Sherlock responded, "Did you hear that, Watson? I am apparently quite well known before I am even born."

"But you don't exist!" I exclaimed in frustration while pointing directly at the stranger. "King Arthur and the Knights of the Round Table, Camelot, Excalibur, that entire story is just that, a *story* based on legends and myth. *"The Idylls of the King"* is just the most recent retelling of it by our former Poet Laureate, Tennyson. It is based on Thomas Malory's *"Le Morte D'Arthur,"* which itself is based on earlier versions by Robert de Boron and Geoffrey of Monmouth's *"History of the Kings of Britain"*. They are all just stories, nothing more!"

"Merlin predicted that you would say that." He nodded, going on. "He also said to tell you that you have been very sick for the last two days with a cold."

"I am sure anyone could guess that just by looking at me!" I interrupted him.

"Caused by repeated soakings in cold seawater during your dalliances with a mermaid named Luna aboard a vessel named the *"Nautilus,"* which somehow travels underwater. He did not explain the details of the underwater ship. Do such things truly exist in this time?"

How on earth could this stranger have known that? Sherlock and I had not told anyone about Luna or the *"Nautilus"*. We had not even left the flat since we returned from our last adventure.

Turning to Holmes, he continued. "Merlin also said to tell you, Sherlock Holmes, that you store your pipe tobacco, whatever that may be, in an old Persian shoe. You acquired your Stradivarius, which I believe is a musical instrument, for a mere 55 shillings, and when you play it, you are, in truth speaking to an ethereal musical Pixy for whom you have a heartfelt longing and wish to meet once again. Merlin did mention that as this quest may take us into the Realm of the Faerie, it could quite possibly lead you to her and be the answer to your wistfulness."

For the second time that day, Sherlock and I looked at one another in disbelief. How could he have known any of these things? Maybe there was something genuine to this odd stranger.

With a glimmer of hope in Sherlock's eyes for the first time in days, he gestured towards a chair and said, "Maybe you had better take a chair and tell us your entire story."

With a deep sigh, the knight walked over to the chair, picked it up, and asked, "Where would you like me to take it to, good sir? We have limited time before we must begin our journey."

Sherlock shook his head negatively and replied, "What I meant was, please sit down and make yourself comfortable while you tell us how you came to be here and what it is you want me to do."

He set the chair down, sat in it, sighed impatiently, and replied, "I came here through a portal in an ancient formation of standing stones, and I want you to come with me to Camelot and locate Alfred Lord Tennyson. It is really most simple. Now, may we be on our way? The gateway is only open for a limited amount of time."

With an enthusiasm in his voice, most likely because of the possibility of reaching the true source of the music that was endlessly calling to him, Sherlock asked, "Can you explain this portal you speak of? Where is it located? How does it function? How did you get from the portal to Baker Street?"

I looked at Sherlock and said, "Holmes, you don't really believe him, do you? Yes, he inexplicably knows more than a few highly personal facts about us that no one could possibly guess, much less know, but there has to be a logical, rational explanation, other than he just walked out of a poem or somehow traveled through time. There always is. Just the other day you were able to look at the map of a cavern you had never seen before and know exactly which room, out of dozens, a prisoner would be held in. And before that, you knew that I was not going to invest in a South American gold mine just from the chalk on my finger. You should be able to see right through this fraud."

Sherlock looked at me and replied straight forwardly, "What I see Watson, is that he does know several facts which would be impossible for anyone outside of the *"Nautilus"* crew and ourselves to know. And based on my monograph *"Determining a Persons Occupation Through Observation of Obvious but Typically Overlooked Characteristics,"* I see that he also is wearing clothes of a weave and fabric that have not been used for centuries. The scar on his forearm was clearly caused by a broad sword, while the scar on his cheek is the result of a glancing blow from a chain mace wielded by a left-handed person. His gait, when he crossed the room to pick up the chair, indicates he is an accomplished equestrian, spending one and a half hours per day in the saddle. The way he holds his left arm is indicative of one used to holding a shield. He has abrasions on his ears from a helmet rubbing against them. Everything I see tells me that he is truly a medieval knight with knowledge of us that is not readily explainable."

The stranger's eyes widened and he exclaimed, "Forsooth! You must be a great wizard also to know such things about me. Merlin stated that your skills in observation and deduction are beyond compare. That is why you must come with me. The standing stones that contain the portal are in the vicinity of a village called Wiltshire. The passage way only opens for a limited time and then it closes. It is invisible to anyone who is unaware of it."

"You say it is near Wiltshire. You must mean Stonehenge, the ancient circle of megaliths that is thought to be a burial site and an astronomical calendar," stated Sherlock. "It is said that standing in the exact center of the circle one can see the sunrise directly over the heel stone on the summer solstice."

The knight's smile broadened and he replied with great enthusiasm, "You *do* know the location I refer to! It is indeed a place of great power. Besides being a portal from our time into yours, it can also be an entrance into the Faerie Realm. We fear that Alfred Lord Tennyson may have unknowingly wandered into, or has been lured into, that mystical land. Its call is difficult to resist, much like the ethereal Pixy Music that enchants your thoughts. We know not where he has gone. Merlin predicted that your far seeing ability will be able to find him, but the nature of your skills demand that you examine his lodgings to do so. We must be off to the standing stones."

I pointed out, "But Wiltshire is ninety miles from London. It would take us several days at least to get there," then with a wink towards Sherlock, I added, "unless we travel via Unicorn, and I am certainly not looking forward to another high speed Unicorn journey any time soon. Our Wonderland adventure had more than enough of those."

Just as I said that, there was a loud clattering of hooves in the hallway, and a majestic white Unicorn paraded into the parlor. With a proud toss of its head, it asked, "Did someone call me? Is it finally time to depart? It certainly took you long enough to convince them. I can't wait to return home to Camelot. This is the strangest quest we have ever been on, Sir Percival. While you were conversing with the wizard and his apprentice, I perused the vicinity of their village. They have great smoke-belching metal beasts harnessed to whole lines of carriages. And they feed the beasts black rocks. I have never encountered anything like it."

"That would be a train pulled by a steam locomotive, also called an "iron horse". And I am not a wizard's apprentice; I am a practicing doctor," I replied.

The Unicorn nodded his head towards me with his spiral ivory horn emitting a silvery glow, and answered, "When you are done practicing, will you be a fully fledged doctor? How soon will that happen? Why do you call that beast an "iron horse" when it does not, in any way, resemble a horse? It looks more like a large furnace encased in a suit of armor with wheels attached to it. And it makes the most horrible screeching sound. How do you stand it?"

I tried to explain, "The name would be a reference to the *horsepower* of the machine, or the equivalent number of horses it would take to do the work of it not actual horses. And "practicing" is the term we use today for doctors that are actually working in the field doing medical work."

"The Unicorn tossed his head again, replying, "But you are not out in a field, you are here in this rather comfortable interior accommodation."

Sherlock interrupted, "We do not have time for discussions on how the English language has changed over the centuries. Sir Percival, how exactly did Alfred Lord Tennyson travel to your world or time period, and what can you tell me about his disappearance?"

The knight turned his head at an angle as if looking for a way to answer Sherlock's question. "Merlin understands it better than I do, but he did give me information that I can share to try and explain. I do not fully comprehend it, but I will do my best.

"The story of King Arthur and Camelot is genuinely true but dates back to a time before history was written. It was remembered and told and retold, sung by bards, troubadours, and minstrels. It was, or I should say is, the history of our life. It is going on right now as we speak. Merlin the Enchanter was born of a human mother and a supernatural father, and due to the nature of his birth, he has great abilities, including the gift of seeing into the future. That is how he discovered you, Sir Wizard. He only uses his powers for good and as a counselor to guide the King. He saw that history would go through a very dark time, and much of what has occurred in the past will be forgotten or be considered to be mere legend and myth. Our entire existence would be considered merely stories. Can you possibly imagine what it is like to know that your whole life will be just a collection of stories and fables to be told as an entertainment?"

Sherlock looked at me and commented, "Imagine that Watson. If the future had to rely only on your overly exaggerated and romantically fancified versions of our exploits, they would imagine me to be some type of super detective rather than the plain and simple practitioner of the highest level of logical observation and rational deduction that I am."

The knight ignored Sherlock's comment and continued, "But there have been those rare individuals whose perception is such that they see beyond your visible world. They can actually see the Faerie Realm. It is somewhat similar to the way that you are hearing the echoes of Pixy Music. You have become attuned to that realm. In your own time, there is another who is very much connected to the

Faerie world. His name is Arthur Conan Doyle. Do you know of him?"

When the knight had mentioned Pixy Music, I noticed a subtle change in Sherlock's demeanor, as if pangs of joy and sorrow enveloped him simultaneously. Although he said nothing, I could sense his longing desire to be with her.

"These gifted ones can sense the real truth of the past. Merlin has been able to reach out and touch those individuals and impress upon them the histories of Arthur and Camelot so they can be recorded for the benefit of your civilization. That is why the stories of Arthur and the Knights of the Round Table have been told and retold over the years by different authors in your world. As you said, Alfred Lord Tennyson is just the most recent of those with the vision of Camelot and King Arthur. He was the one chosen to record it for your generation."

"So what exactly happened when it was presumed that he had passed away?" Sherlock asked.

"Merlin said to say that it was exactly like the method you used in the Grinning Cat Adventure to pass from your realm to the reality outside of time, except that it did not require a circle comprised of real and imaginary creatures and beings, only the Unicorn. And he did not pass outside of time, just to an earlier time. And there were no questions from the Time Guardians. And it was permanent and not just a temporary state. But beyond that, it was entirely identical. Regarding Sir Tennyson, I believe that you are aware of the Unicorn's healing powers."

At that moment, the Unicorn interrupted, pointing his spiral horn at me and said, "If you would like a demonstration, I could take care of that cold for you very quickly. You will feel entirely better."

I was about to accept his offer, but Sherlock interrupted, "When Alfred Lord Tennyson passed on, his entire family was with him at his bedside. How could they not have noticed anything unusual?"

"Yes, that is true, but as you are aware, and as your scribe has recorded in your previous adventures, the swiftness of the Unicorn is almost beyond perception. When Sir Tennyson's time for passing was imminent, with just a minor distraction, the Unicorn was able to replace him with an identical looking fabrication created by Merlin, and at the same time, Alfred Lord Tennyson was healed by the Unicorn's spiral horn. No one noticed a thing"

The Unicorn once again pointed his horn at me. "The *proper* term for my horn is '*Alicorn,*' and I *really* could help you with that cold."

I was again about to accept, when the knight carried on with his story: "With a minor disturbance outside the room and the swiftness of the Unicorn, it all occurred so instantaneously that no one was able to realize a replacement had been made. It is not the first time that people have been switched. I believe the French author, Alexander Dumas, is going to write a tale about a man in an iron mask which involves something of that nature. I can't imagine why anyone would wear an iron mask. Do you have any idea what my helmet weighs?"

Not waiting for a response, he went on, "You are aware that Alfred Lord Tennyson was very melancholy. He is remembered as being one of the saddest poets in history. That is because his true desire was Camelot. *"The Idylls of the King"* was written based on his personal observations during his visits there, except for the conclusion of

11

course. That was fabricated just to provide a moralistic end to the story for the readers of your time. All of the conclusions that have been written are made up. That is why there are variations in all of the different versions written over the years. Arthur is still alive in the time that I come from. Our lives have not yet come to an end. Sir Tennyson visited Camelot on many occasions, and he was his happiest during those times. That is why he was so melancholy when he was back here in your own time."

The knight paused and, with a sad look in his eyes, explained, "As he lay dying, he whispered a wish to visit Camelot one last time. Merlin granted him that wish, and as a result, he was also healed by the Unicorn. Sir Tennyson was brought through the portal so he could visit Camelot in appreciation for his efforts in keeping us alive in your memory. That is how he came to be in our time period."

"But what about the Time Guardians?" I asked. "How was he able to avoid them when he traveled into the past? If you have traveled through time to get here, then you know all of time travel is controlled by them. We met the Guardians during the Grinning Cat Adventure, and would not choose to cross paths with them again."

The knight hesitated a moment, glanced down at the floor, and then looked up, almost as if embarrassed, and replied, "Merlin predicted that you would ask that question. The portal in the Standing Stones is a shortcut that bypasses the Time Guardians. He did not have to answer their riddles. But it only works when traveling to or from Camelot, so it does not create a great many problems.

"Alfred Lord Tennyson, having written twelve epic poems about King Arthur, was well suited to live in our time. When he arrived in Camelot, he sighed, and said that at last he was home. He prospered and was happy, which is why we are concerned for him. We do not believe he would have willingly left Camelot of his own accord. That is why I was sent to seek you out, Sir Wizard. You have the ability and far seeing vision to find him."

Before anyone could say anything else, the Unicorn added, "And I have the ability and the Alicorn that can cure you, Dr. Watson."

To which I quickly replied, "Yes! Please, before any one says another word!"

Chapter 2.

A Very Odd Journey, (And without question, the absolute best cure for a cold.)

The Unicorn gently lowered his spiral horn and touched my forehead, and in a glowing instant, my cold was gone. In truth, every ache, pain, soreness, and even fatigue had vanished. I had never in my life felt better than I did at that moment. It was as if a wave of healing, silver light passed over me, and when I emerged from it, I felt more alive than ever before. Every fiber of my being longed to bask in that feeling forever.

The Unicorn tossed his head back letting his flowing main flutter as if in a soft breeze. "Yes, I am aware I would make a most excellent doctor. I have heard that sentiment many times before. But just as you are a doctor, not a wizard's apprentice, I am a Unicorn and not a doctor. It is my nature." Turning to Sherlock the Unicorn added, "But I am sorry to say that, as powerful as my Alicorn may be, it cannot relieve what ails you Sir Wizard. There is but one cure, and should you accompany us, Merlin believes that your destiny is to meet the one whose music dances endlessly in your dreams and haunts your days."

"Either way, I thank you sincerely..." I started to say, but before I could continue, Sherlock interrupted. "Yes, yes, now that your cold is out of the way, let us return to the matter at hand. If Merlin can see into the future well enough to have located me, and knows what awaits me and what I am longing for, why can he not locate Alfred Lord Tennyson? Considering his powers that you have alluded to, it should be simple for him, unless some force is blocking his abilities, or Sir Tennyson has passed into a realm not visible to Merlin."

The knight's eyes grew wide in amazement, and he replied, "Your perception is astounding, Sir Wizard. That is exactly why Merlin cannot find him. Normally Merlin can sense the presence of Lord Tennyson but something is blocking his vision."

Sherlock pondered a moment and answered, "Yes, that would also be a possibility. You are correct, Sir Percival. It appears that we do need to visit your time period to determine what happened to Alfred Lord Tennyson. However, if we are going to accompany you into the past, we will require suitable attire. I believe we would be rather conspicuous wearing 1890's clothing."

"Thank you, Sir Wizard. I have brought robes for you both in my traveling pack. You can wear them over your current clothes if you desire. But I must ask you, is your attire actually comfortable? It appears you are being strangled by those silken cords around your necks."

Not waiting for a reply, the knight reached into a leather rucksack and produced two brown woolen robes with rope cords to secure

15

them. Sherlock and I donned them, but not before Holmes performed a quick navigation of the room picking up various items from the shelves and tables and then depositing them into his coat pockets. Standing in front of me, with a contemplative look on his face he addressed me: "My dear Watson, you look like a character out of "*The Legend of Robin Hood.*" My instincts tell me that your service revolver could prove very useful in this adventure, but we cannot risk bringing a modern weapon into the past without the danger of altering history. That is the one thing we *must* avoid, so we will have to make do with these."

He handed me a sturdy walking stick that looked old fashioned enough, and for himself, held up an antique sword he had produced from some hidden corner of the room. After adjusting his robe, setting the sword belt securely on his hip, and gazing sadly in the direction of his pipe, he commented, "We must also leave this behind, Watson. It is another contrivance of our time that would be out of place in Camelot."

The Unicorn replied, "In my perusal of the area surrounding your domicile, I saw several men partaking of those odd devices, and they were spouting more smoke than those iron horses that eat the black rocks. It cannot imagine that it is at all healthy. Why would they do that?"

Ignoring the Unicorn's question, Sir Percival proceeded to explain the plan. "Unicorn will first take me to the portal and then return for the two of you. Merlin mentioned that you are both experienced in the wonder of travel via Unicorn…"

I must admit, upon hearing that, I was nearly sick at the thought of another high speed Unicorn journey dodging trees at blinding velocities, but I did not interrupt Sir Percival.

"…and how it is near instantaneous. However, I do have to ask if either of you are prone to sea sickness or nausea. It has been mentioned that riding a Unicorn at high speed is comparable to being at sea in a great storm, in small boat, with the wind blowing from all directions all at once."

At that point, the Unicorn did interrupt the knight with a proud look. "I assure you I am not at all comparable to a small boat. I am merely the fastest creature on four legs and much faster than most any winged creature."

Ignoring the Unicorn Sir Percival carried on, "And then I will lead all of us through the portal. As I mentioned, it is invisible to those who do not know of its existence. Shall we be off to Camelot?"

At that point, the Unicorn then Sir Percival blurred and vanished from the room. Realizing that it might be quite some time until my next cup of tea, I leaned forward towards my tea cup on the table, only to find the Unicorn suddenly materializing beneath me.

I abandoned all hope of any tea and desperately wrapped my arms around the Unicorn's neck and closed my eyes in fear. After a good deal of wind rushing by I chanced to open my eyes, to see one very close call with a large stone monolith. Soon I found myself standing in field next to Sir Percival. Sherlock was examining one of the standing stones with his magnifying glass and commenting, "This is extraordinary, Watson! For all practical purposes this megalith appears no different than any of the others, yet it is a doorway to the past. That is unfathomable, yet it must be so. Shall we be on our way? The game is most definitely afoot, as we will certainly not find any trains where we are headed."

The Unicorn snorted and replied, "If you mean those rock-eating, smoke-belching, metal behemoths, I say good riddance. I would rather face a real fire-breathing dragon any day."

My eyes grew wide as I looked at Sherlock and asked, "Did that Unicorn just say there are real *fire-breathing dragons* where we are going?" Sherlock gave me a push through the portal and answered, "I am sure it was just a metaphor, Watson, just a metaphor."

It was as if reality turned inside out. I felt like my body was being stretched until it snapped, and suddenly I was again standing next to the stone beneath a full moon. Holmes was commenting, "You know, Watson, with these most recent adventures, I have enough material to pen a monograph on *"A Study of Phase Transitional, Chronological, Temporal Transportation, and its Practical Applications"*. What do you say, old boy?"

I was too utterly terrified to answer, as I was looking directly at a scaly red dragon less than two feet away from me!

I was, of course, quite relieved when I realized it was only a realistic painting of a dragon on a shield that happened to be in front of me. The knight, whose shield had given me such a fright, was talking to Sir Percival.

"You have returned, Sir Percival, and in truth, you have brought visitors. Pray tell, is this the Wizard and his apprentice that Merlin predicted would find Sir Tennyson?"

I recovered my composure and interjected, "That would be Consulting Detective and Doctor, if you do not mind. I am Doctor John Watson, and this is the famous and apparently timeless, Consulting Detective, Sherlock Holmes."

The Unicorn interrupted saying, "If you think their speech is strange, their attire is even stranger, and they have the strangest mechanical dragons in their time period."

The knight looked aghast, and he exclaimed, "Mechanical dragons? Forsooth, Sir Wizard, why would one create such a creature? Knowing real dragons as I do, I would imagine that it would be near impossible to control."

Sherlock looked at me and under his breath responded, "Considering how poorly trains adhere to the published schedules, he is not far off in his concerns."

He turned to the knight who been waiting for us and said, "It is a pleasure to meet you, sir knight. You need not worry about combating mechanical dragons. We did not bring any with us. I see by your attire that you have already recently encountered white tailed deer, brown bear, wolverine, and wild boar." Turning and addressing our guide, he continued without even taking a breath. "Now Sir Percival, shall we proceed directly to the lodgings of Alfred Lord Tennyson, or are we to meet first Merlin the Enchanter?"

Chapter 3.

A Very Odd Encounter, (And a clever rhyme as well.)

"By Faith!" cried the new knight. "Indeed I have. Pray tell, how is it possible for you to have known all this when you have just arrived? Do you possess the far sight or is it the evil eye?"

He looked at Sherlock suspiciously, and he placed his hand on the hilt of his sword, slowly backing away from him until Sir Percival stepped in. "Fear not, Sir Bedivere. This wizard possesses skills in observation and deduction that are far beyond compare. He and his apprentice doctor friend have come hither to help us."

"But Sir Percival," stated the Unicorn, "Doctor Watson is no longer an apprentice as he is now here in this field and not residing in his comfortable domicile."

I thought about trying to explain the difference, but decided against it, as it would have been futile. In truth, I was astonished by the environment we found ourselves in. The standing stones which surrounded us seemed to be almost alive. They looked much younger and less worn than I remembered them to be, which made sense, as we had somehow traveled centuries into the past. The fragrance of the area had a natural, musky earthiness to it, much like an autumn forest after a rainfall. It was as if the entire surroundings were alive in a primordial way. Most noticeably, the stillness of the night was profound. The noisy clatter of London and all of its bustle and activity were gone. There were no sounds around us other than crickets and the occasional frog.

Sherlock broke the silence by explaining to the knight how he had known what he did. "Sir Knight, my skills are neither magic nor sorcery: they are acute observation, plain and simple. I was able to tell the last four creatures you encountered by looking at you and your surroundings. It is quite obvious that you have strands of white tail deer hair on your sleeve; there is a recent tear on the shoulder of your tunic that could only have been caused by a bear claw. The wolverine gives off a distinct odor which is still on your person, and there is a roast of wild boar cooking on your campfire over there. As I stated, it is all observation."

"Indeed, it must be, Sir Wizard," the knight said as he relaxed his sword hand. "You are as gifted in seeing as Merlin. And as of late, he has only been speaking in riddles and prophecies."

"But if I am correct," Sherlock replied, "he has predicted that I will locate Lord Tennyson and also meet the one whose music is haunting my dreams. Let us be on our way to see him. Which direction are we going?"

"Which direction indeed?" A deep voice suddenly echoed from out of nowhere and continued:

"Follow your feet,

and you shall meet,

the person you seek,

but do not be weak.

East is the least,

West is not best.

North will not lead forth,

and South is uncouth.

So what do you say

upon this day?

Do you know

wherefore to go?"

Sherlock, looked up into the night sky, and replied, "Merlin, you are here with us now. If we need not travel in any direction, then I deduce you are already here. Based on the direction of the echoes and the audible volume of your voice, I believe you are behind *that* stone."

Sherlock spun on his heels and pointed directly at one of the medium sized standing monoliths to the left of us. From behind it stepped an aged wizard with long grey hair and an even longer grey beard. He was wearing a deep blue robe tied with a gold cord, and he carried a gnarled wooden staff that appeared to be an old tree branch, which had the appearance of a dragon's head on the top of it. His most striking feature, however, were his eyes. They were the deepest, clearest, and brightest blue that I had ever seen. They looked as if they could see into eternity or into one's soul.

"Well done, Sir Wizard.

By my gizzard,

you have detected well.

Come sit for spell.

I will tell you why

beneath the night sky,

you are here;

because mystery is near."

"I do understand that," replied Sherlock. "This entire adventure is a mystery, but we are here, so tell us what has happened. Sir Percival has explained how Alfred Lord Tennyson was healed and came to be here in Camelot. Apparently, I am to discover where he has gone, and what has become of him. Tell me. What occurred over the last six years between his arrival and his disappearance? Did he have any enemies in Camelot? In what condition was his health? Was he inclined at all to wander far away? Who were his companions? How did he spend his time?"

From within his robe, Merlin produced a glass vial, held it up and swirled its contents, as he spoke.

"Memories of time gone past,

fleeting things that still do last

witness here, the poet's life,

you will see there was no strife.

Memories of time now flown

Captured as the years have grown

Look and listen, and you will see,

where the poet perchance may be."

As he finished speaking, with a wide sweep of his arm, he turned the vial upside down and poured the contents out of it. Much to my surprise, the liquid did not just spill to the ground; it formed a cloud, or a mist that hung in the air before us. Upon the cloud were images of Alfred Lord Tennyson living in Camelot. It was as if daguerreotypes of Tennyson were printed directly on the misty cloud. We saw him walking among the people of Camelot, having meals with them, telling them stories, writing poems, and more. Merlin was somehow showing us scenes from the life of Sir Tennyson since he had left our world. We had observed his peaceful and harmonious new life for quite some time when the image showed Sir Tennyson standing in front of a doorway with his hand on the door knob. The next image showed him looking back towards the direction from which he came, as if he knew he was being watched, and wanted the watcher to see him entering the room. The next image showed him turning back to the door and entering the room, followed by a picture of a completely empty room. As the mist faded and cleared, Merlin again spoke.

"He passed through that door

and then was no more.

The room you can see

Is quite empty.

Wherefore did he go?

You must learn and know.

By the great dragon's bones,

Tell us Sherlock Holmes."

As Sherlock contemplated, I stared at the empty space where the images had somehow been displayed. How on earth had Merlin been able to do that, I wondered.

Sherlock finally responded, addressing Merlin, "How soon can I inspect that room? Has anyone been in there since he disappeared? How is it that you capture and display the images we just watched?"

Merlin smiled softly and answered.

"What you see,

comes from me

What I view,

I show you.

That very room,

Is like a tomb.

No one would dare

Go in there.

For you to see,

Follow me.

Let us now go,

And you shall know."

As he finished speaking, he turned and strode away from the circle of stones using his dragon staff as a walking stick. Sherlock and I followed, accompanied by the Unicorn and the two knights. I asked Merlin how long it would take us to get to our destination, and his response, while detailed, left me less informed than before he answered. In his simple rhyme he had responded,

"How long indeed?

What is your speed?

How fast you go

Tells what you want to know.

The distance traveled

Can be unraveled

Look to the sky.

Do not ask why.

When the sun eats the moon

We will be there soon.

When the time is right,

Thus ends our flight."

Sir Percival chimed in, "Now you see what I mean about talking to Merlin. Pray tell, how does King Arthur make any sense out of Merlin's advice? I would have gone daft ages ago."

Sir Bedivere then nudged him and interrupted, "Gadzooks! This is being stated by one who travels in the company of not just a Unicorn, but one with the gift of speech?"

Percival responded, "You may gad about my questing companion, but we have been to the future and seen their mechanical dragons. And we have brought hither the Wizard and his apprentice doctor. It is said that he can see the invisible!"

I was about to comment, when the Unicorn waved his Alicorn and said, "You are all aware that we could already be there if you allowed me to provide the transportation."

Merlin abruptly halted, turned to face the group, and stated,

"Verily indeed

we require speed.

The beast is right.

He will aid our flight."

Then turning directly to the Unicorn, he went on.

"If thou please,

the moment seize.

To make haste there,

we are in thy care."

And with that, first the Unicorn, then Merlin blurred and disappeared, followed by Sherlock and Sir Percival.

"And I shall keep watch over the horses and meet you there," sighed Sir Bedivere.

Meanwhile, I closed my eyes and braced myself for yet another high speed Unicorn ride dodging trees, stone monoliths, and in this time period, who knew what else. The Unicorn materialized beneath me, and fearing the worst, I wrapped my arms around its neck and held on for dear life. There was a sudden, brief rush of wind, and then I heard the Unicorn's voice announcing, "If you please, you can stop strangling me now, Dr. Watson. We have safely arrived. Your Wizard friend is already examining the premises. Based upon your reaction to the incredibly unique and most honored experience of riding upon a Unicorn, one would perceive that you do not enjoy it. Pray tell why is that?"

"It is because, on several occasions, I *have* experienced breathtaking Unicorn rides at speeds beyond my imagination. I still wake up at night from nightmares of near collisions with trees that are trying to jump in front of us."

"Well, yes, that would explain it," the Unicorn answered. "There are those of our species that relish the experience of traveling faster than the wind, even if it does involve an occasional near miss with a tree or two or, in *very* seldom instances, having to pry one's horn from the trunk of a tree. We try not to mention those occasions when that does happen."

My eyes grew wide when I heard its last comment, but Sherlock was already voicing his observations on the last location of Alfred Lord Tennyson. "Yes, he was at the entrance to this room. Based on the images of him that you showed me, I can deduce his height, weight, shoe size, the length of his stride, and a slight limp, and there are matching footprints going up to the door. But if you look closely, you will see they do not enter the room. There is a clear indication here of when he stopped and turned to look back. It is as if he wanted to give the impression of going into this room and make sure that your observation of him showed him doing that, but I assure you, if you look closely, you will not see any footprints entering this room. It is as if it never happened. I penned a monograph on "*Determining Direction and Misdirection in Footprints Based on Readily Observable but Typically Invisible Attributes.*" This is a classic example of misdirection in footprints."

"But how could he just disappear from here?" I asked. "Could a Unicorn have whisked him away? I have no familiarity with the workings of this time period."

I looked to Sir Percival and Merlin for answers, but Sherlock continued to examine the ground in front of the doorway using a magnifying glass he had taken out of one his pockets and answered. "As nebulous, transitory and quick as Unicorns have proven to be, they do leave evidence of their prior presence no matter how brief it is."

The Unicorn lifted his head with a puzzled expression, turned towards Sherlock, and remarked, "Is that true? I had no idea. Pray tell what evidence would you be referring to? Would it by any chance, be the radiant silver glow of my Alicorn that remains after I have graced an area? Or, could it be the unmistakable aura of magic that follows me where ever I go?"

Sherlock pointed to the doorway with one hand and to where Merlin was standing with the other and explained: "It is much simpler. You see where you deposited Merlin, there are very slight traces of Unicorn hair, and the ground is slightly disturbed from your hooves. The same holds true for where Sir Percival is standing. But in the last location where Sir Tennyson was seen, there are no indications of a Unicorn's presence."

Sherlock entered the room to continue his examination. While he did, I looked through the doorway myself to see what might be in there. It was a simple accommodation with a bed and small table along one wall. There was a writing desk and chair near the adjacent wall, which also held several shelves full of scrolls. The third wall had a fireplace and what looked like a basic kitchen facility of that era. A slightly larger table with chairs around it filled the center of the room. Sherlock stood just inside the doorway, turning his head slowly, looking around the room and taking it all in, when he suddenly stopped and turned back to one of the shelves. He walked over to it and examined a glass vial very carefully with his magnifying glass. After a moment, he gestured for Merlin to come into the room and inspect it.

"Merlin, does this vial contain the same substance that you used to show us images of Sir Tennyson? The residue is the same color and thickness as the contents of the vial that you used."

The aged enchanter ambled over to where Sherlock was standing and replied:

"Far you see,

Farther than me

Yes indeed,

The answer is freed.

It was not him

That did not go in.

Only a shade,

of him was made."

"Astonishing!" I exclaimed. "But who would have the same skills as Merlin to be able to create such an illusion? And why would they do such a thing? It was obviously intentional to prevent anyone from seeing where Lord Tennyson actually went. But, who would do such a thing?"

Sherlock bent down to the floor in front of the shelf. He picked up something that was invisible to my eyes from where I was standing, studied it, and the ground in front of the shelf, stood up again and answered, "The last person to hold this vial before we arrived was female, tall, slight in stature, and had long copper colored hair. Can any of you tell me who that might be?"

With a look of concern and wonderment in their faces, Merlin, Sir Percival, and the Unicorn all answered in unison, "Morgan la Fey!"

Chapter 4.

A Very Odd Realization, (And the discovery that one plus one does not necessarily equal two.)

I thought for a moment and realized his conclusion was not at all logical. I asked Sherlock, "But how could it only be an image when you discovered his footprints going right up to the doorway. If he was not really there, then where did the footprints come from? And where did they go from here? How could there be both real footprints and an illusionary image? It does not make sense."

Sherlock looked at me and nodded. "That is an excellent question, Watson. That is the point! You are getting more observant. That is exemplary, but you miss what is behind the obvious. Two different clues clearly tell us that he did not enter the room; the image vial and the footprints that stop at the doorway. They both say the same thing, but they contradict each other. Either one by itself would provide the required proof that he did not enter the room, but both of them together, irrefutably prove he really did enter this room.

"Whoever left the clues wanted to be certain that one would be found but did not count on both of them being discovered. Look at that ceiling beam. Its position provides the perfect anchor for one to use a rope to swing from the doorway to directly in front of this bookshelf without leaving any footprints. If you look closely at the beam, you will see there are rope fibers caught in the grain of the wood. Sir Tennyson's footprints appear again right here alongside the female's foot prints. And from this point, both sets actually do disappear completely. Now that I have explained what happened here, can any of you tell me who is Morgan la Fey, and why she invokes such concern?"

Before anyone could answer, Sir Percival exclaimed, "But pray tell, you did not explain what happened, Sir Wizard. You clearly illustrated how he could have moved from the doorway to the book shelf without leaving footprints and that Morgan la Fey was standing next to him here, but where did they go? In truth, how could they both have vanished?"

Sherlock paused and enjoyed another of his immensely favored theatrics, those moments when he, with great flair, unveils the hidden secret that only he knows. He casually asked, "Is it not obvious? This bookshelf is actually a doorway to a hidden chamber behind it. They passed through the secret entrance which is why their footprints seem to have vanished."

He then slowly ran his finger over the top edge of the shelf until he reached a particular spot, at which he stopped, exerted a slight effort which produced a clicking sound, and the shelf swung back into a dark recess that revealed a stairway leading down to who knew where?

Indicating caution, Sherlock held up his hand, and again reiterated, "However, before we descend into the dark, forbidding, unknown abyss before us, I would like to know more about the owner of this domain. What can you tell me about Morgan la Fey?"

The Unicorn, who was still standing outside the room, stamped his hoof and responded, "Well, that would depend upon whom you ask. Even though she is Arthur's half-sister, and at one time was a gifted student of Merlin, there are those who view her as a villain and an enemy of King Arthur and Camelot. Others see her as the heroic protector of the Faerie Realm. She is fighting to prevent magic from disappearing. Arthur, however, is a harbinger of change. In his poems of Camelot, Lord Tennyson often quoted King Arthur's very words, *'One age passes to make way for the next.'* He feels that change is inevitable. Morgan la Fey is using her powers to prevent the age of the Faerie Folk from vanishing into myth and legend, just as Arthur is striving to keep the vision of Camelot alive as history devours the present. It is indeed a paradox." Tilting his horn in my direction, the Unicorn looked at me and added, "Although what *'two* doctors' have to do with the problem at hand, is beyond my powers of comprehension."

"Fie!" exclaimed Sir Percival, "It matters not how many doctors are involved! Morgan la Fey is a powerful enchantress who has used her abilities to vex Arthur many times. In truth, she is an enemy of the kingdom!

"But how can that be?" I asked. "As the Unicorn stated, and according to the stories I have read, Morgan La Fey is Arthur's half-sister. But he has no magic. So how can she be a powerful enchantress? And why would she be against Arthur, and why would Arthur be against the Faerie Realm when he has Merlin himself, the most well known wizard of literature, at his side, and one of his own Knights of the Round Table travels in the company of a Unicorn."

Merlin laughed and voiced,

"Why indeed?

The forces are freed.

You must see

beyond her and me.

She and I

are like the sky.

Dark in the night,

but in the day light.

Yet still the same

in nature and name.

Look and you'll find,

we are ever entwined."

Sherlock responded in frustration, "Mysteries and rhymes are all we are getting out here, Watson. I suggest we simply go and see where this passage leads. It cannot be any more unusual than what we have already experienced in this odd adventure. And I am certain the answers to Lord Tennyson's disappearance, as well as where I might find Pixy Music, are through this door."

With great apprehension and recollections of similar predictive statements that proved considerably otherwise, I entered the room and prepared to follow Sherlock into the secret chamber and wherever it would lead to.

As he passed through the doorway, I heard him call back to me, "Cheer up, Watson old boy, this is no different than the monograph I wrote on, *'Determining the Correct Direction of Travel at an Ambiguous Crossroads by Eliminating the Obviously Incorrect Directions Through the Use of Rational Logic and Deduction'*."

Then Sherlock Holmes vanished before my eyes!

Chapter 5.

A Very Odd Set of Rules, (And an even odder resolution.)

What on earth had just happened? Sherlock was there and then suddenly he was gone. We all looked at each other in disbelief. Was this another portal? I was about to ask Merlin when much to my surprise, Sherlock reappeared in the doorway, saying, "Are you coming along, Watson? You really have to see this. It is quite remarkable."

And then he disappeared again. Relieved to see Sherlock, and trusting in his judgment, I made up my mind to follow him. Without hesitation, I entered the doorway and somehow found myself standing in a wooded glen. Sherlock was standing nearby examining the ground and commenting. "It is as I suspected, Watson, the two sets of footprints came through the doorway, out of the portal, and they head off in this direction. And if my senses do not deceive me, which they rarely do, I believe we are in the Faerie Realm. Let us be after them."

The hidden doorway had been a portal of some kind, and I gazed in amazement at where it had taken us. We were in a clearing within a small circle of moderately sized standing stones that was surrounded by a wide variety of trees and shrubs. The trees soared up to the sky, casting a soft shadow over the entire area, except for the sunlight that filtered through their branches in fluttering rays blinking in and out as a slight breeze played in the limbs. A rainbow kaleidoscope of flowers in every color and type grew in abundance, many of which I was certain I had never seen before. It was a botanical paradise. If this was the Faerie Realm, I could understand why Morgan was trying to keep it alive, but I did not see any of the danger that Sir Percival had warned us of. It appeared to be the most peaceful and entrancing place I had ever visited.

My thoughts were broken by the arrival of Merlin, followed by the Unicorn who announced as he appeared, "Sir Percival will wait on the other side of the portal. He stated that he will prevent any unwanted intruders from following us, but I believe he is hesitant to set foot into the Faerie Realm. It is said that few who enter ever return. In looking around I understand. Why would anyone want to leave? It is most inviting here."

In an impatient tone, Sherlock pointed upward through a slight break in the branches and voiced his opinion: "I could provide a dozen reasons without even mentioning the large dragon-like creature that is circling above. We are here to find Alfred Lord Tennyson, and I feel in my heart that Pixy Music is somehow connected to this place. I cannot explain it but I know she is here somewhere. For the first time in days I feel alive again. My only regret is that I did not bring my violin. How will I be able to speak to her?"

"I am sure you will find a way." I optimistically answered.

"Yes, I am certain I will. I know with all my heart that I must." and he pointed towards a pathway. "The footprints lead off in this direction."

Glancing up into the sky, I followed him and inquired, "Don't you mean the *metaphor* that is circling above?"

Merlin ambled towards the path, saying to no one in particular.

"Dragons fly,

while pathways lie.

Secrets to know,

so let us now go!"

The Unicorn followed Merlin, gazing to the left and to the right, commenting on the beauty that surrounded us. Sherlock, at home in his element of following a trail of clues, no matter how impossible or improbable the environment, walked along the pathway stopping to examine trifles that would have been invisible to anyone else.

"The two of them passed by here only days ago with the female leading the way," he called back to us. From several feet down the trail, he called out again, "They stopped here to rest and were joined by a multitude of very diminutive beings. The creatures, while sporting human-shaped feet, were impossibly smaller than any I have ever encountered in the past. Their visitors apparently vanished without leaving any discernible footprints leading away that I can detect, another oddity in this adventure, and then the two of them continued on in this direction. A different breed of creature with larger and less human looking footprints followed them for a time but wandered off in that direction." Then with a shortness of breath and an excitement in his voice, he whispered to me, "And even more promising, Watson, is that I *hear* her. I can feel the echoes of Pixy Music more clearly than ever before. Every one of my senses tells me she is somewhere in this land. Her music is imbued in the earth, floating in the air, ringing in the trees, and surrounding me like a golden glowing cloud. I know I will find her. It is only a matter of time..."

With a nod, the Unicorn commented, "Your sorcerer friend sees very well. Most humans would never notice the Faerie Folk if they were right in front of them, much less seeing evidence of their previous presence."

My mind reeled as I tried to grasp the implications of what the Unicorn was saying. Based on Sherlock's observations, this place was populated by beings known only in fairy tales and myth. Who knew *what* we would encounter next?

The answer came in a deep booming voice that emanated from somewhere up ahead on the path, "None shall pass!"

A heavily armored dwarf sporting a beard reaching all the way down to the ground was sitting upon a large rock alongside the pathway. His armor looked well-seasoned, and in addition to the large axe he held up to bar the way, he must have had at least a half a dozen additional weapons hanging from belts and chest straps. I would not say that he was unsightly, but I will say he strongly resembled a large furry dog that had been stuffed into a miniature suit of armor. He repeated more adamantly, "None shall pass!"

Sherlock, not in the least bit concerned, walked right up to the imposing figure and addressed him. "Those are the rules, Sir Dwarf, none shall pass?

The dwarf shook his axe threateningly and responded in an even louder voice, "NONE SHALL PASS!"

Sherlock simply replied, "Then do your duty and let us pass, my good dwarf. My companions and I are all called *'None'*."

The dwarf laughed heartily and responded, "A most clever ruse, you trickster. If you are all called 'None', then what be your surnames?"

Without hesitating, Sherlock answered boldly, pointing at Merlin, "This is the Wizard, None Too Tricky." Then pointing in my direction, he continued, "Here is my associate, None of Your Concern; the Unicorn, None Too Modest; and allow me to introduce myself. I am None of Your Business."

I nearly choked when I heard his response, but the dwarf was apparently pleased, and with one hand, he casually swung his axe and buried the blade in a nearby log saying, "I give way to 'None'. You may all pass! Give my regards to the Lady in Green."

"I shall give her your regards and let her know that you are doing an admirable job. Most passable indeed!"

The dwarf retrieved his ax from the log and called out, "There are none that sneak past me!"

I caught up to Sherlock and whispered, "That was very clever, Holmes. How did you come up with that idea so quickly?" He answered with a grin. "It was 'none too challenging,' Watson, quite elementary, actually. It is only a matter of observing and assessing the situation and taking the most logical approach."

"Logical?" I replied incredulously, "There is nothing at all logical about this adventure. The next thing you know a knight in shining white armor will be blocking the road and challenging all who want to pass, to a duel."

Sherlock nonchalantly dismissed my comment. "Don't be foolish, Watson, you should know that all knights blocking paths and demanding a duel are attired in black armor."

Of course as soon as we rounded a bend in the road, there was a tall knight in pitch black armor, blocking the road and demanding a duel.

Chapter 6.

A Very Odd Duel, (With just a bit of trickery on Sherlock's part.)

"I challenge ye to a duel!" the knight declared as he threw a gauntlet to the ground, "Declare your choice of dueling implements!" At that moment, the tall fearsome figure pointed to a weapons rack containing numerous different swords, axes, maces, flails, spears, halberds, and other even nastier looking implements of death and dismemberment. The situation looked most assuredly bleak. While Sherlock was skilled in fencing with foil and saber, the weapons the knight offered were of a completely different nature.

Holmes, however, walked past the weapons rack and pointed at the small repast of mead and biscuits that the knight had sitting on a large flat stone and replied, "I choose mead and biscuit dueling."

"What?" the knight incredulously responded. "That is my noon meal, not a dueling weapon. What trickery are you trying to accomplish here?"

Sherlock held his ground and pointed at the meal replying, "I am following your directions and choosing my dueling implement as you demanded. You pointed in this direction and said 'choose'. I choose mead and biscuit dueling. Of course where we come from, it is typically *tea* and biscuit dueling, but the most civilized beverage ever to grace this country has not yet arrived in England, so mead will have to suffice. Do you accept my choice of dueling implement, or do you forfeit the duel?"

The Black Knight stood silent like a great statue in obvious disbelief before he replied, "I have never before engaged in a duel with mead and biscuits. I typically just eat my biscuits and then drown them in ale. They don't fight back. You will have to explain the rules of this odd duel."

He then removed his helmet, set it on a log, and with great powerful steps, strode over to where Sherlock was standing. "I am Sir Bruin, the Black Knight. Any party who wishes to pass must engage me in a duel, but I do not comprehend how biscuits and mead may be used as dueling implements."

I gazed at the knight as he stood awaiting a reply. He was massive in stature and looked as if he could snap a tree branch in two without even trying. His hair was black and straggly and his eyes were deep and dark. There was a base primal air about him. I wondered if the array of weapons were his trophies from previous contests.

Sherlock, undaunted by the imposing presence of the knight, sat down on a log near the mead and biscuits and pointed to an empty space across from him. "Move a rock here, and sit down. It is cool under the trees here. I will explain the rules. Dr. Watson, you will officiate"

The knight picked up a large stone, and with a loud thud that shook the ground, placed it opposite Sherlock. In truth, he looked as if he could have crushed the rock into pieces if he had wanted to. Sherlock pointed at the mead and biscuits. "It is quite simple really; we will each have a cup of mead in front of us. Dr. Watson if you please."

I found an extra flagon and set it in front of Sherlock, as the knight had already had one for himself. I set the plate of biscuits in between them. I filled each of their vessels to the brim and set the mead down to see what Sherlock had in mind, as I myself, had never heard of tea dueling or, in this instance, mead dueling.

"It is quite straight forward, actually," Sherlock explained. "We each take a biscuit and dunk it into the mead while Dr. Watson counts to ten out loud. At the count of ten, we each remove our biscuit and hold it as long as possible before eating it. If it falls apart prior to being eaten, then the opposing contestant is awarded a point. The first one to attain five points wins. As I stated, it is most simple. You try to postpone eating your biscuit as long as you can without it falling apart. Do you have any questions?"

The knight looked at Sherlock with a disappointed expression and exclaimed! "That's it? Just ale and soggy biscuits? No swords, daggers, axes, flails, or maces? Not even spear throwing? What kind of duel is this? Upon my honor as a knight, I demand something more challenging!"

Sherlock stood up and removed a dagger from his belt and held it up. "All right, something more challenging it is. Take a biscuit and throw it up into the air."

The knight looked confused and asked, "What kind of challenge is that?"

Sherlock made an exaggerated gesture pointing upwards towards the trees with one hand, while he held his dagger at his side with the other and replied, "Just throw a biscuit up there; that is if you are able."

Upon hearing his ability questioned, the knight harrumphed and grabbed a biscuit from the plate and heaved it upward. With an incredible swiftness, Sherlock hurled his dagger upward also, and in an instant, his dagger fell back to the earth with the biscuit impaled on its blade.

Sherlock pointed at the skewered biscuit, picked up a new one, prepared to throw it into the air, and stated, "Now it is your turn. Is that challenging enough for you, Sir Bruin?"

The Black Knight's eyes grew wide with amazement, and he exclaimed, "Forsooth! I have never before seen such speed and skill with a dagger. I yield to you, sir. You and your companions may pass."

Sherlock picked up his dagger, removed the biscuit, and casually tossed it up into the tree saying, "Well then, we will be on our way. Enjoy your biscuits and mead. The highest I have been able to count before eating a dunked biscuit is up to sixty. Do give it a try and see if you can match that. We may pass this way on our return trip."

And with that, we made our way past the knight who was busy dunking his biscuit into his mug of ale and counting out loud while glancing up into the tree wondering why nothing had fallen back to the ground.

If it is possible for an equestrian creature to snicker, then I would say the Unicorn was most assuredly doing so as we continued on the path. When we were far enough along the path not to be heard, it addressed Sherlock, "You are not only a master of observation and deduction, Sir Wizard; you are also marvelously adept at sleight of hand. I saw what you did there. You distracted the black knight by pointing up into the trees, while you impaled a biscuit on your dagger *before* you threw it. That was most clever of you. But how did you know the biscuit he threw would not come back down along with your dagger?"

Sherlock smiled and replied, "Ah ha! Now that was the truly clever part. I positioned us beneath the trees, because I knew the creatures hiding up there would grab the biscuit he threw into the branches but would certainly avoid one with a dagger impaled on it."

The Unicorn nodded, "Oh yes the Brownies that were hidden in the leaves watching. I am surprised you noticed them. They are all but invisible to humans."

"I see everything. Of course I noticed them. And according to folklore, they do like biscuits. I convinced the knight to toss his to them, and they did not bother mine while it was impaled. That is why I tossed the biscuit back up into the tree after I removed it from the dagger. The brownies were quite cooperative, and it all worked out very well."

Merlin then chimed in.

"Very well,

time will tell.

You won the day

with your play

of sleight of hand

and a band

of creatures rare

in the air."

"That was brilliant, Sherlock." I stated. "The magicians at the hippodrome can't hold a card to you, but telling him that you have held a dunked biscuit for sixty seconds? Don't you think that was going too far?"

Sherlock looked at me with a wry grin and replied, "All right, so I neglected to mention that it was a week old stale biscuit. It will keep him busy trying."

Chapter 7.

A Very Odd Creature, (And without question, the most outstanding music I have ever heard.)

While Sherlock was following the footprints, I wondered what would be in store for him if he did actually encounter the source of the enthralling music that that filled his thoughts and desires. He had certainly not been himself over the last several days. He would play his violin for hours listening intently to her echoing reply, and then gaze silently out the window. I knew where his thoughts were. They were off somewhere in a far distant realm, longing to be close to her. But now in this strange and enchanting land, she was closer, but still no nearer than before. The anticipation must have been unbearable for him. Who knew what we would encounter next?

We had been traveling for some time down the path under the shade of the trees when Sherlock came to a sudden halt. The forest had thinned out, and we were about to pass into an open area.

"Why have we stopped?" I asked. "Is it another Black Knight or a dwarf blocking the path? I don't see anything."

"That is because you are not looking in the correct direction," he offhandedly replied pointing upwards. "You may want to look up there, although that is not to say things are looking up."

I could not believe my eyes! Through the clearing that had opened in the trees, I spotted a large, scaly green, winged creature circling above. It had sharp pointed claws on both its front and hind legs, large leathery wings, and a long lizard like tale. The face had a look of ancient wisdom and cunning cleverness and was almost handsome if you ignored the teeth and horns. The eyes were a deep gold and seemed to burn with an intense fire. There was no question about it. I was looking at a genuine, real dragon!

"What was that you were saying about metaphors?" I turned and asked Sherlock. "Now what do we do?"

The Unicorn however, seemed not to be afraid and boldly walked into the clearing, raising his head and calling out, "Greetings, Malachite the Musical!"

The dragon turned its head towards us and swooped down to land in the path very lightly considering its size. In the sky, it had been impressive, but upon the ground standing before us, it was positively fearsome!

In a booming voice that sounded somewhat like a harpsichord, which as you know has often been described as a keyboard instrument that creates musical notes with a mechanical twang on the end of them, the great beast bowed his head and replied, "Unicorn! It is pleasant to see you again. And you bring visitors as well. This must be the time of year for guests. Morgan La Fey passed through here only days ago. It was fortunate she had a poet with an excellent singing voice along with her. You do remember the rules for passage through my domain in the Faerie Realm."

As I heard that, I whispered to Sherlock, "Not another challenge to travel down this path! And I thought the toll roads in our time were outrageous. This beats them all hands down."

The dragon slowly turned its head towards me and, with a smile that was more frightening than friendly, laughed, "Apparently your traveling companion is not aware of how sensitive a dragon's hearing truly is."

The Unicorn quickly responded, "Indeed, Malachite, they have just arrived in our land. They are not familiar with the customs and have never met a real dragon before, not to mention, one as musically gifted as you."

The dragon responded by playfully blowing a puff of flame into the sky and singing up and back down again the notes of the musical scale. "Well, in that case, I can excuse them, but that still does not change the rules."

Sherlock stepped forward and with a flourishing bow addressed the beast. "We thank you for your consideration, green and great maestro. If you would explain these rules you allude to, we would appreciate it. I deduce by what has already been stated they pertain to, us providing some type of musical challenge or an amusement. I myself have some small musical skill and may surprise you."

The dragon's smile was, I imagine, clearly meant to be friendly and, I am sure meant to display some degree of happiness, but it was like looking into the teeth of a half a dozen buzz saws.

"Outstanding!" He declared. "It is verily quite simple. For your group to pass by, one of you must provide some type of musical performance that is new, novel and unfamiliar to me. The poet accompanying Morgan La Fey sang an impressive epic song about a charge of a cavalry light brigade. It was stirring but sad. I am only 100 years old, so I am certain that there are still a few songs or types of musical entertainment that I have not yet heard. Since you have not brought any instruments with you, you may enter my cave over yonder and choose one that is suitable. I do have an outstanding selection. Yes, I know, most dragons tend to hoard gold and jewels, but to me, music is so much more valuable than gold or any of those precious rings you hear about. Truthfully, as gold must be first smelted and poured and then polished to attain its brilliance, it does not hold a natural beauty to me. Music on the other hand..."

Malachite did not finish his sentence but instead seemed to be lost in profound contemplation on the wonder and beauty of music. Indeed, he seemed to be conducting an imaginary orchestra with one of his fore claws. This was assuredly not what I had expected in a dragon; however as certain as I was regarding Sherlock's musical skill, we were somewhere in the sixth century, and the violin had not yet been invented! How was he going to resolve this challenge?

Merlin and the Unicorn waited with Malachite while I accompanied Sherlock into the dragon's cave. I expressed my concern regarding what he would use since there were no violins in this time period. The instrument, as we know it, would not appear for another thousand years.

"Fear not, Watson," he replied. "While the violin of our era may not be present, I am certain that we will find a bowed stringed instrument that is close enough to suffice. You may not be aware, but I recently penned a monograph on *"The Evolution of Stringed, Bowed Musical Instruments, and Their Effect on Civilization, With a Focus on Their Involvement in Criminal Activities."* In gazing around, I am confident that I will find what I am looking for."

The dragon's cave was astonishing! Musical instruments of every kind filled the cavern. There were many types of lyres, harps, lutes, horns, trumpets, bagpipes flutes, tanburs, and more. Many types of instruments I had never even seen before were present and some simply defied description. The collection that surrounded us would easily put any museum in London to shame.

Sherlock stood perfectly still gazing about the space and taking it all in. His eyes darted from left to right as he analyzed the available choices and considered his options. Music had evolved considerably since the sixth century, would he be able to find something that worked? The dragon had not been clear, or for that matter, even mentioned the consequences of not producing an acceptable musical performance. Recalling his toothy smile and claws, I chose not to consider that possibility.

Sherlock, however, seemed quite pleased with himself. He had found a bow and an unusual odd-shaped stringed instrument that seemed to somewhat resemble a violin, even if the body shape was totally wrong. "Ah, yes," he said aloud. "This will do just fine." And he exited the cave.

The dragon turned his head at an angle as he considered what Sherlock had retrieved from the cavern. "What have we here? You selected a bow from an ancient Greek lyre and a smaller early four-stringed fretless lute known as the barbat. That is an interesting combination. I am intrigued. This may be quite fascinating."

Sherlock proceeded to tune the instrument he had selected, and the dragon twisted his neck to observe the process even closer.

"Hmm,… G, D, A, and E. That is an interesting tuning. I have never heard that particular combination before. Where did you come across it?"

Sherlock stared longingly into the distance and wistfully replied. "It comes from a musical instrument that does not yet exist in this time, the violin. But the melody that I am going to play is timeless and will remain close to my heart always. It is, both simple and profound; deep, yet unfathomable. It is beyond words or description, yet it speaks volumes. It is enchants me endlessly."

Malachite nodded his head in acceptance and sighed, "Ah, a love song. Those are always pleasing. You may begin when you are ready."

While the diminutive lute was not at all shaped like a violin, it was small enough for him to tuck under his chin. I must say, it was certainly an odd-looking contrivance. But the sound that came out of it when Sherlock drew the bow across the strings was once again magnificent. I instantly recognized the haunting and mystical melody of Pixy Music that I had first heard on our way back from Wonderland and again aboard the Nautilus when Sherlock had played Captain Nemo's Stradivarius. Through the beguiling tune, he had somehow connected to the ethereal creature, Pixy Music. It had been echoing endlessly in his mind since he had heard it, and now he was embracing it. The melody he played was moving, like a playful breeze that dances in the trees, drawing you ever onward. It teased and whispered softly, then called loudly. It was bold and shy, bright and gentle. It was captivating beyond description.

Once more it sounded as if a duet was being performed, with Holmes playing the melody and Pixy Music playing the harmony. Impossible as it was, we heard two distinct and separate musical lines dancing playfully together even though there was no one but Holmes playing. She was reaching out and touching Sherlock with her song, and he was responding with all his being. The melody was truly alive with warmth and passion and energy.

Merlin and the Unicorn closed their eyes to let their senses flow with the ethereal, enchanting music to wherever it would take them. Their heads were swaying and nodding gently to the enrapturing song. The dragon, however, stood as still as a statue, his eyes opened wider than it seemed possible, glowing as brightly as if they were on fire. His entire being seemed to be consumed in the song. I noticed a slight fluttering in his claws as if he too, was accompanying them in the mesmerizing tune. Entrancing and hypnotizing, the music continued until it softly came to a halt echoing briefly. And then all was still.

It was not until that moment that I noticed a tear in the dragon's eye. Malachite twisted his neck downward so that he was level with Sherlock's eyes. He stared intently at him for just a moment, bowed his great head, and finally spoke. "That was more than a mere love song. It was pure rhapsody, a love duet that transcends time, distance, and worlds. You have gently touched the mystical Pixy Music, and she has in turn, sweetly caressed you. I will remember this day forever. You may go forward. Your destiny is waiting."

Chapter 8.

A Very Odd Development, (And a clarification on swords, which of course, Sherlock had already written a paper on.)

Sherlock was about to set down the odd instrument and bow when the dragon added, "I am honored to have heard and experienced such ecstasy. Please, keep the lute and bow with my sincerest thanks. They are my gift to you. No one could ever bring them to life in the way you have, and I foresee you will need them again before your journey in the Faerie Realm is concluded."

Holmes bowed his head in acknowledgement and replied, "Thank you, Malachite. It has been an honor, but we must be on our way."

As we started towards the path again, I glanced in the direction we were heading, and I would have sworn that there were a multitude of fantastic mythical creatures gathered there in rapt attention. I blinked and looked again, and they were gone. I turned to the Unicorn, who was walking next to me, and asked, "Did you see that? What were those creatures?"

The Unicorn slowly nodded and replied, "Yes, I did, and I am not surprised. Your friend has clearly announced his presence in the Faerie Realm. His duet with Pixy Music was heard by not just Malachite and ourselves. Music resonates in ways humans have not yet begun to understand. I am sure that now all of the Faerie Realm is aware of Sherlock Holmes' connection to Pixy Music.

"But what does that mean?" I asked. "How will that affect our effort to find Alfred Lord Tennyson? Does that help or hinder us?"

Merlin, who had been silent up until this time, chimed in.

"What indeed?

Meaning is freed.

Their songs proclaim

with great fame.

Sherlock is here,

Pixy Music is near.

Go forth now

and somehow,

time will tell

all is well.

You will see

what will be."

I turned to Sherlock and asked, "And *what* exactly is that supposed to mean? If Merlin is Arthur's counselor, it is no wonder he was unaware of what is happening here."

Sherlock responded with a sigh, "Do you not see it, Watson? It is obvious. As illogical and improbable as all of this seems, you must examine it for what it is and deduce the implications. Like Wonderland from our Grinning Cat adventure, this is a realm beyond our normal rules of science. When I play the melody that I first heard in Wonderland, and Pixy Music accompanies me, we are communicating. Her music resonates beyond normal physical limits. The other faerie creatures of this time can also hear it. I imagine Morgan le Fay is also well aware of our presence by now. Yet somehow Merlin sees that in the end, it will work out well."

"And so it shall," a soft female voice replied from somewhere nearby. We turned to look, and there we saw a white-haired maiden in a shear light-blue satin gown bound lightly by a silver chain. A circlet of fine silver held back her long hair. If it is possible, her eyes were even deeper and bluer than Merlin's. She was not overly tall, and while she did not appear to be old, there was a gentle look of wisdom in her gaze and smile. A necklace of sea shells adorned her graceful neck. I thought to myself, could this be the legendary Lady of the Lake?

Merlin's eyes brightened when he saw her. With his arms outstretched he quickly strode over to where she had appeared, and exclaimed,

"Nimue, my child,

come to me!

Here in the wild

How can it be?

Did you forsake

your watery home,

and leave the lake

all alone?"

They embraced warmly, and she replied, "You have taught me well, dear Merlin. My form can briefly be here, while my spirit is still in the lake, but I must not tarry. I do long to see you again." Looking in the direction of Sherlock, she added, "Your Wizard friend exquisitely announced his presence and his connection to the aerial musical Pixy, so I knew you were near. Bring your traveling companions with you. I have news of the poet he is seeking. When you reach the lake, we shall once again enjoy a moment together. Until then, my dearest Merlin…"

The maiden held out one hand as if to say farewell and then faded away into a nebulous mist. "That was astonishing!" was all I could say. Merlin meanwhile stared into the mist and replied,

"Goodbye my dear.

Return to thy lake.

Do not fear,

I will not forsake

the love we share,

timeless and true,

endless and rare

ancient and new."

The Unicorn, with a nod of his horn in the direction of the road asked, "Did you hear that? The Lady of the Lake has information on the whereabouts of the poet. That is promising. Shall we be on our way?"

We all continued down the path, and I asked, "So where exactly is the body of water that is her home? I have heard of her in the stories of Camelot. I believe she is the one that gave Arthur his legendary sword, Excalibur. But I thought he withdrew it from a stone."

Sherlock cleared his throat and whispered to me, "Watson, if you had read my little monograph, *"A Brief Synopsis of All Formally Named, Historically Important Swords and Their Influence on History,"* you would know the answer to that question."

Since I had not read his paper, the Unicorn filled me in on the details, and with the air of a lecturer, he held his head high, and responded, "Well, first, 'the lake' is known as Dozmary Pool. It is down the road a short distance. The sword that Arthur removed from the stone to claim his kingship has often been confused with Excalibur, but they are two separate and unique weapons. The first sword was placed in the stone ages ago with the prophecy *'Whoso Pulleth Out This Sword of this Stone and Anvil is Rightwise King Born of all England.'* Arthur achieved the throne by doing so and then uniting the warring minor kings.

"He received Excalibur, also called Calibourne, from the Lady of the Lake early during his rule. While the sword is mighty, even the scabbard has great power. It can heal wounds and prevent blood loss. It is almost as powerful as I am. I sometimes wonder if an Alicorn was used to make the scabbard, but I know the Lady of the Lake would never do such a thing."

I nodded and inquired, "If I may ask. What is the relationship between Merlin and Nimue? They seem quite close."

The Unicorn turned his head towards Merlin who was spiritedly walking along the path with a pleasant smile on his face then looked back to me. "Yes, they are more than close. They are soul mates. She is one of the Queens of Avalon and the Guardian of the Lake. She watches over the watery realm, similar to the way that Morgan La Fay watches over the Faerie Realm but without Morgan's animosity. Merlin has been teaching her all of his enchantments and has grown quite fond of her. I have heard him say that he will be hers forever. He is completely enamored.

"Morgan la Fey is terribly jealous of them and was furious when she found out. For many years, Morgan had also been a student of Merlin, excelling in all of the arcane talents, nearly equaling him. She had, at one time, fancied herself as being close to him, but it was not to be. In her anger, she cast an enchantment on Merlin that prevented him from speaking, so he could not communicate with Nimue. But Merlin found a way around the spell by speaking in rhyme. The heart of a poet is one of true love and always finds a way."

I smiled and replied, "It sounds very romantic, but what do think she meant by she has news of the poet we are seeking? Do think she had anything to do with his disappearance?"

The Unicorn shook his head negatively and responded, "No, of course not. That is less likely than the scabbard of Excalibur being made of Alicorn. While Arthur is working to move England forward, he does respect the land and waterways. The Lady of the Lake gave him Excalibur to aid in his task. She knows the poet is important to Arthur and Camelot. She would never harm Lord Tennyson."

Merlin, meanwhile with an energy and nimbleness that defied his age, made his way towards the lake home of Nimue all the while reciting a love poem.

"Nimue, my dear…

Every road it leads to you

no matter where it goes.

This is certain. This is true.

My deepest heart it knows.

To the mountains frosty air

to walk in snowy fields

amidst the ancient beauty where

my heart to you it yields.

To the timeless ocean blue

and the salt sea air.

My heart it longs to be with you,

and my love you're there.

Within the emerald forest tall,

the silence and the peace,

I hear but one true endless call.

My love will never cease.

Though I travel far and wide

to places close and near,

I long to feel you by side

to hold you close my dear.

Like a beacon burning bright

a loadstone sure and true,

your love it is an endless light,

leading me to you.

You're ever in my fondest dreams.

You're all my heart's desire.

Every path and way it seems

it longs to lead me higher.

Higher, deeper, farther too,

I know that it is so.

Every road it leads to you.

This my love I know."

As he finished reciting the poem, a body of water loomed in the distance not far ahead. Merlin stopped abruptly and starred as if he sensed something was wrong. I was about to ask him, when he suddenly pointed and exclaimed,

"Unicorn, to the lake!

For Nimue's sake.

We must make haste!

No time to waste!"

First the Unicorn, and then Merlin, blurred and disappeared, reappearing near the shore in the distance. Sherlock then vanished and reappeared standing next to him. I closed my eyes and prepared myself for another terrifying ride at speeds beyond comprehension being thankful there were no trees or stone monoliths along the way. I felt the Unicorn materialize beneath me, and wrapped my arms around its neck. The next thing I knew I was standing in a foot of water near the shore while Merlin and Sherlock were standing on dry land only a short distance away from me.

I looked first at the Unicorn and then down into the water, and with a toss of his head, he stated, "You do realize, that near instantaneous travel is not an exact science. At least there were no trees or stone monoliths here to get in the way."

Sherlock meanwhile was already closely examining the area and flatly stated. "It is as I suspected. Morgan La Fey and Alfred Lord Tennyson were here earlier. Their footprints are clearly visible."

Merlin with a look of great sadness, turned and responded,

"It is worse than that.

Where she is at

I cannot say.

Morgan's taken Nimue."

Chapter 9.

Another Very Odd Realization, (And an even odder explanation from Sherlock.)

Sherlock, while still looking down at the ground, declared, "Morgan was here with Sir Tennyson two days earlier. They continued off in that direction," and he pointed to the north, "but then she returned by herself only moments ago. There was a struggle near the shore, and then she vanished from the area somehow taking a portion of the lake and shoreline with her. My deduction is that some type of sphere of containment was cast around Nimue also capturing a segment of the shore and the lake. Morgan apparently transported the sphere to another location. However, we are in luck. Prior to being taken captive by Morgan la Fay, Nimue was able to leave us a message."

Taking several steps away from the shoreline, Sherlock pointed at a random grouping of shells and rocks and commented, "If you look closely, you will notice that the sea shells over here are arranged in very specific way. The shells that are right side up spell out a message. 'Look under Round Table.' It is obvious that Nimue discovered some bit of information, and she was able to communicate that to us in time."

I looked at him and asked, "So now what do we do, continue on the trail of Morgan and Lord Tennyson or follow this new lead regarding Nimue? I imagine that the Round Table she is referring to is back in Camelot."

"Indeed it is," interjected the Unicorn. "It is located in Arthur's grand hall. I cannot imagine how there could be a clue or a message hidden beneath it. The Round Table has been a central part of Arthur's rule since he assumed the kingship. It conveys the message that all the knights who sit there are viewed equally. All discussions regarding what goes on in Camelot occur there.

"But if I understand correctly, Morgan La Fey was not included in those discussions, and that is why she is resisting Arthur and why she has taken Tennyson," Sherlock replied.

The Unicorn replied, "Truthfully, we do not even know if she has 'taken' him. He may have gone with her willingly. She can be very persuasive."

"But I believe that is unlikely," answered Sherlock. "From what I have learned so far, Alfred Lord Tennyson was devoted to Arthur and Camelot."

Merlin, who had remained silent since discovering Nimue was gone suddenly spoke,

"Enough of this talk.

Let us now walk.

If four becomes two

we will find what is true.

Two paths remain.

We have much to gain.

It must be so.

Let us now go."

Sherlock looked up and replied, "He is correct. We could make more progress if we split up. Merlin and the Unicorn could go the court of Camelot and search underneath the round table while Dr. Watson and I continue along the trail. With the speed of the Unicorn, they could be there and back in almost no time."

The Unicorn held up his head proudly and answered before Merlin could reply, "At last there is someone who truly appreciates the speed of a Unicorn. I will have Merlin there and back most expediently!"

First the Unicorn and then Merlin blurred and vanished, leaving Sherlock and I utterly alone in a very odd land. With them gone, it was as if our safe connection to the place had disappeared, and the strangeness seemed to intensify a hundred fold. It felt like dozens of hidden eyes were watching us from the mists. It was as if we were surrounded by unseen beings that whispered and pointed at us. I was certain I could hear strange voices chattering somewhere nearby. I was frozen in my tracks and was about to say something when Sherlock tapped me lightly on the shoulder saying, "Well Watson, let us be on our way or they will be back before we have even moved. We do need to make some sort of progress while they are gone, if we are to live up to my reputation here."

Hearing Sherlock undaunted by the situation brought me back to my senses and broke the spell that had seemed to have come over me. I looked around and nothing was out of the ordinary. The placid waters of the lake looked like any other body of water and the surrounding area once again appeared quite normal. I passed it off as only a side effect of my imagination getting the best of me and began walking behind Sherlock as he strode off along the pathway that followed the misty shoreline.

"Their footprints are as easy to follow as if they were leaving sign posts!" I heard him call out as he hurried down the road, stopping here and there to examine some near invisible trifle that caught his eye. I quickened my pace to catch up to him, and was nearly there when he turned to me and asked, "So Watson, did you happen to notice the odd little creatures that were watching us whispering and pointing when the Unicorn and Merlin left? I think they may have been some of the same beings that had gathered to listen to the musical interlude that I played for the dragon."

I stopped in my tracks and stared at him. "What did you say? Are you saying that there really were a multitude of mythical beings there, that it wasn't just my imagination?"

He glanced at me with an incredulous look and replied, "You would need a good deal of imagination to conjure up some of the inhabitants of this place, Watson. Faeries, Pixies, Brownies, Gnomes,

Goblins, Silkies, and those are just the ones that are relatively friendly."

I shook my head in disbelief. "Sherlock, I cannot believe that is you talking. Are you not the one who said that your detective service is firmly grounded in reality? No ghosts need apply! Prior to these most recent adventures, you would have dismissed all of this as shear fantasy and nonsense. You would not have even considered it. Yet here we are wandering around 'Faerie Land' with a fictional wizard and a talking Unicorn on a mission for King Arthur to locate a poet who actually died six years ago. And you are more than hoping you are going to encounter the nebulous, ethereal Pixy whose music is haunting you!"

"Yes, Watson, perhaps that realization is more than a bit odd. I will grant you that. But as I have explained many times earlier, sometimes even the most improbable situation can turn out to be the truth when you eliminate everything else. I am sure when this is all over and we are back in our flat, you will remind me of this adventure when we are faced with some other equally minor perplexing conundrum."

"Good sir, pray tell, we are dealing with not only the disappearance of Alfred Lord Tennyson and the Lady of the Lake but the revelation of a secret chamber hidden beneath the Round Table of Camelot! A secret listening chamber in the King's own meeting hall! I assure you, this is not a minor concern, if that maketh what a conundrum translates to in your time."

Sherlock and I quickly turned to look to where the deep, baritone voice had come from. There standing next to the Unicorn, who had returned without our noticing, stood a tall, well-built, dark-haired knight who radiated confidence, success, and ability. His very posture spoke of skill and victory in all knightly endeavors. He was proud and

71

somewhat arrogant, yet there was a sadness to his countenance as if all of his success meant nothing.

"I am Sir Lancelot, the Right Hand of King Arthur and champion of his Queen Guinevere and the victor of countless tournaments," the knight proclaimed. "When Merlin and the Unicorn returned to Camelot and urgently instructed us to look beneath the Round Table, we thought he was jesting. 'Merlin,' the King declared, 'What are you saying? Are you making joke? We already have a court jester. Why would you have us look under the table?' but he was most insistent. When we discovered the hidden chamber, the King sent me to inform you."

Sherlock looked up as he pondered Lancelot's words and quickly responded. "Tell me about the listening chamber. Have you found the passageway from some other nearby location that leads into it? If I am correct, there are small female footprints and strands of long copper colored hair present, possibly the fragrance of certain herbs and forest plants."

Lancelot's jaw dropped and his eyes grew wide. "Yes, yea, and yea verily! Pray tell, how is it possible for you to know such things when I just arrived and have not yet told you? The room was somehow hidden even from Merlin's sight."

The Unicorn nudged Lancelot and whispered, "I told you he would know everything you were going to say before you stated it. He is truly a great wizard."

Sherlock shook his head negatively and answered, "There is no magic in my abilities. It is merely the highest possible level of observation and deduction. Based on the obvious, I believe that Morgan La Fey has been listening to all of Arthur's plans and decisions as they are being made. She is possibly even influencing matters subtlety using herbal means. There are certain herbs and botanical compounds which if diffused into Arthur's meeting chamber, would cause a myriad of unexpected effects. That could explain her advantage and how she was able to lead Lord Tennyson away."

"By the Sword of Arthur, and my reputation as the greatest knight of Camelot, she shall pay for this!" thundered Lancelot. "None shall stand before me..."

"I did say *possibly* influencing matters, Sir Lancelot," interrupted Sherlock. "While I am quite certain she has been listening, I am not absolutely positive that she has been using means to adversely affect Arthur and his knights. From what I understand, she is only trying to keep the Faerie Realm from vanishing, just as you are striving to protect Camelot."

Lancelot was about to reply when a puzzled look came across his face, and he paused briefly, looking to the left and right as if trying to determine what to say in response. After a moment, he firmly gripped the hilt of his sword and continued in a loud voice, "But I am Sir Lancelot, the Right Hand of King Arthur, the champion of Queen Guinevere, the victor of countless tournaments, and the defender of Camelot. I cannot abide by Morgan La Fey's interference. Something must be done!"

Sherlock quietly held up his hand to calm Lancelot "And I assure you something is being done, Sir Knight. Did you per chance discover where the passage leading from the chamber went to? That will possibly tell us something useful."

"That is the strangest thing, Sir Wizard. The passage from the chamber under the table led to a dungeon cell, the very one she somehow escaped from many months past."

When I heard that, I could not restrain myself and exclaimed, "Arthur had his own half-sister put in a dungeon? What on earth for?"

Lancelot turned to me and responded, "She had burst into the Round Table chamber and boldly threatened to kill the King and Guinevere in front his entire court. Arthur tried to reason with her, but she was insistent, she said the only way to stop her was to imprison her. By faith, of course she was imprisoned to protect the King and Queen. Arthur made certain her cell was quite comfortable, but after only five days, she had disappeared from the prison cell. It was still securely locked, but empty. She had somehow vanished. The chamber we discovered beneath the round table led directly back to that cell. The entrance from the cell to the passage was cleverly hidden, and not discovered until moments ago."

I looked at Sherlock and asked, "What do you say Holmes, do you think the threat to kill the King and Queen was just a ruse to gain access to that room in the dungeon so she could create a passage to the round table?"

Nodding affirmatively, Sherlock replied, "Indeed Watson, your perception is increasing. But the question is how did she then escape from a locked cell? My conclusion is that she was hiding in the listening chamber, and it only appeared completely empty, so it was left unlocked. She was then able to return to the cell and leave in disguise. After that, she could come and go dressed as one of the workers. No one would pay attention to her, so she had unlimited access to the cell and the chamber beneath the round table. Or she may even have a servant working for her. It was quite clever actually."

"But what are we to do, Sir Wizard? Arthur has posted guards at the cell and in the Round Table meeting chamber. What do we do next? By the Towers of Camelot, we must do something! You have the Sword of Lancelot, Champion of the Queen, and the Right Hand of Arthur at your command!"

Sherlock quickly responded, "Then return at once, and remove the guards. Leave the cell unlocked. Return the Round Table to its original position, and instruct Arthur to call a meeting of all his knights."

If it were at all possible, Lancelot looked even more surprised by these directions than by Sherlock's previous revelation, and he interrupted, "By faith! You would have us leave the cell and access to chamber unguarded? Forsooth why?"

With a wry smirk, Sherlock elaborated, "Instruct Arthur to use this meeting to read the provisioning list, the laundry list, the tax records, anything that will keep the gathering going as long as possible."

Turning to the Unicorn, he asked, "Unicorn, after you have brought Lancelot back to Arthur's court, can you return here, and convey me to Camelot? Then I must request that you to return back here to Dr Watson."

Turning in my direction he addressed me. "Watson, when the Unicorn returns, I want you both to continue following the trail left by Morgan. You have accompanied me long enough to know what I am looking for. It is the near invisible, undetermined '*something*' that no one else would see, and if they did, they would pay no attention to. It is quite elementary, actually. If I had a copy of my paper on *"Seeing the Unseen by Looking for the Obviously Invisible With a Focus on the Hidden Trifles,"* you would understand. If do you find anything significant, send the Unicorn back for me. Meanwhile, I have a Round Table meeting to attend.

Chapter 10.

A Very Odd Predicament, (And an even odder bridge, if you can call it that.).

The Unicorn and Lancelot returned to Camelot while Sherlock was assuring me that I would be just fine. He was certain I would find *something*, although he could not say exactly what, but I would know it when I saw it, and then a moment later, he was gone. Once again, the odd feeling of utter alienation returned.

I stood transfixed in silence for a moment, listening and looking for strange creatures or unexplainable beings peering at me through the haze. I was straining to see through a swirling undulating mist that seemed to rise up from the lake towards the land like a giant nebulous octopus, when the Unicorn suddenly appeared in back of me commenting, "We should probably be on our way, you know. During the foggy season, the visibility along the shoreline can be exceptionally limited at this time of day."

I nearly jumped out of my shoes at the suddenness of his return, but I managed to retain my composure and replied, "Yes, that is probably a very good idea. Just out of curiosity, when exactly is the foggy season?"

The Unicorn looked up for a moment pondering and then turned and answered, "I would say all year long or at least for the last several hundred years, as far as I am aware. It could be even longer than that. Either way we should be off."

I cringed at the thought of a foggy season lasting more than several hundred years, and began studying the footprints that meandered along the lakeside trail. Having worked on cases with Sherlock countless times in the past, I had some degree of confidence that I would be able to successfully follow them to wherever they led. My assurance quickly faded, however, as the path transitioned from a soft sand to a harder rocky surface.

"What's this?" I asked out loud as the footprints faded away. "All right, now what do we do?" I stopped and studied the ground looking for some type of clue that would indicate the passage of Morgan la Fay and Lord Tennyson. It was then that the words of Sherlock echoed in my mind: "*Look for the invisible trifle. See what no one else does.*"

"Yes, the unseen invisible…" I muttered.

"Would that be the slight scuff marks on the ground?" I heard the Unicorn ask. "If you look closely, you can see a slight scrape mark there and then again further along. It matches the pace of Lord Tennyson's stride."

I examined the areas the Unicorn had indicated and realized that he was correct. Sherlock had previously mentioned that he had noticed a slight limp in Alfred Lord Tennyson's footprints, and the scuff marks clearly fit the spacing of his stride.

"An excellent observation!" I commented. "You are quite good at this."

"Yes, it is true. Unicorns do have a close connection to the land. I could tell you if even a rabbit passed this way, but your Wizard friend has observational powers that are beyond anything I have ever witnessed."

"Indeed, Sherlock is quite talented." I replied and continued to follow the all-but-invisible trail. As we walked, I asked the Unicorn, "What would Morgan la Fey want with Alfred Lord Tennyson? Did she kidnap him just to vex Arthur? Do you believe she intends any harm to him? Considering his age when he arrived in Camelot, he would be eighty-nine years old by now."

The Unicorn pondered briefly and replied, "Morgan la Fey is passionate about keeping the Faerie Realm from fading away, and she is quite angry with Arthur, but I do not believe she would harm the poet. She admired his works. She is also furious with Merlin, which may explain why she acted against Nimue. But with Morgan, it is hard to understand or say anything. She is quite unpredictable."

After a while, the rocky ground gave way to a softer earth, and the two sets of footprints were once again clearly visible.

"Ah, this is much better." I mentioned aloud, as I pointed to the now clearly discernible trail. "I wonder where this will take us."

By now, you may be thinking that I should have known better than to vocalize such a question, considering where my previous pondering vocalizations had led to on our most recent adventures. But at the time, I was feeling confident and rather sure of myself in following the footprints, and I was clearly not considering what the answer to my question might actually be. Whatever it was, I was certainly not expecting a *sword bridge*!

I have previously read of how Sir Lancelot overcame the near impossible task of crossing a mystical sword bridge in several of the literary retellings of Camelot, but I never imagined such a thing could actually exist. Yet there it was right before us, spanning a deep chasm across a turbulent, raging river. It was an impossibly large sword set lengthwise vertically on end with the sharp edge facing upwards. Although the path led directly up to it and the trail continued on the opposite side, how could it even be called a bridge? No one could cross that and survive. What were we to do?

The Unicorn looked at me and asked, "You aren't expecting me to cross that, are you? Even as swift and nimble as I am, I still require some sort of footing. And you can see the river at the bottom is far too dangerous to attempt a crossing."

I looked to either side of the bridge and saw no other crossings as far as one could see. The gap only grew wider as the distance away from the sword bridge increased, so this was the narrowest crossing point, but how to achieve it? It seemed all but impossible. I looked closer to see how it was supported, and that is when I saw that the hilt of the sword was being supported not by rocks but by a pair of greyish colored knobby hands. Looking even closer, it was then I saw a diminutive creature residing in a depression in the rocks, and holding the sword in place.

"Hello! Who are you? What are you doing in there?" I asked.

A sharp gravelly voice replied, "I am a Kobold. And I am also the bridge keeper. What does it look like I am doing? I am holding up the sword bridge. It should not take a wizard to see that."

The Unicorn stepped forward and replied, "But he is not a wizard; he is either an apprentice or a doctor, depending on where he is standing at any given moment. It's rather complicated actually. I don't fully understand it myself."

Ignoring the Unicorn's comment, I asked the creature, "Why are you holding it with the sharp edge up? How is one to cross the bridge when the sharp edge provides no footing?"

The creature grumbled with sound of rocks scraping against each other and answered, "That is none of my concern. My task is to hold up the bridge, and that is exactly what I do. Not that it is very interesting. "

It was then that an idea came to mind. I whispered to the Unicorn to get ready to quickly take us across when the opportunity presented itself, and then I bent down to look at the creature. It was old and gnarled and did not seem to be very happy with its task.

"I imagine that is so," I said. "It must be extremely difficult. When do you even get a chance to have your meals? You must get very hungry holding up that bridge all day. Are you allowed to set the hilt down at all to eat?"

It looked at me with a surprised expression. "Of course I can set it down when I eat. How else would I be able to otherwise?"

I removed from my pocket, some of the biscuits that I had brought with me from Sherlock's mead-dueling contest, and offered them to the Kobold. "That may be, but would you care for some of my biscuits? They are most delicious, and I would be happy to share them with you."

The creature's expression brightened somewhat as it started to move, and its voice changed from gravely to something more akin to a rusty gate hinge. "Well that is the best thing I have heard you say since you arrived. That is most kind of you."

He set the handle down which caused the sword to rotate ninety degrees so that the flat edge was now facing upwards creating a narrow surface that one could just barely walk upon. Then he stretched and flexed his fingers with a distinct popping and cracking sound. "Some fresh biscuits sound most welcome right about now, perhaps with a good flagon of ale."

I glanced at the Unicorn to get ready, and then set the food on a flat rock near the trail. "Here you go, good sir. Enjoy!"

As the Kobold moved towards the food, I quickly nodded to the Unicorn, and in an instant, he blurred, materialized beneath me, and then took off like a race horse with my arms franticly wrapped around his neck. I tried not to think about the impossibly narrow surface of the sword we were going to traverse, or the consequences of not making it across. However, in less than a moment, we made it across the sword bridge and were making excellent progress down the path on the other side of the ravine, and for once, I truly appreciated the speed of a Unicorn.

Chapter 11

A Very Odd *Something*. (I would not have expected it but knew it when I saw it.)

The Unicorn eventually slowed down, stopped, and I dismounted to examine the ground for clues. As I did, the creature observed, "That was a rather creative approach, even if you did give away your evening repast. But I must say that it was certainly more expedient to cross the sword bridge when it was horizontal than if it had been vertical."

"I am curious,' I replied, "I wonder how Morgan and Lord Tennyson crossed the bridge. Their footprints are clearly on this side of the ravine and they keep going along this trail. How did they manage it?"

We continued following them until *it* happened. It was at that point that the unknown *something* that Sherlock had stated I would find suddenly appeared. Or actually disappeared, so to speak. The two sets of footprints had been clearly visible for quite some distance when they veered towards an exceptionally large oak tree, went right up to it, and totally vanished.

"What's this?" I asked aloud. "Could this be the mysterious *something* that Sherlock was talking about? I *do* wish he were here right about now."

I looked around both sides of tree and tried to see if they continued further down the trail, but I could not see a thing. I looked up towards the branches, but the lowest limbs were a considerable distance up into the tree, and it did not seem likely that a man of Tennyson's age could have made his way up there and safely taken an aerial route through the forest. What could have happened to them? Was this tree another type of portal? This was certainly an unexpected *something*, even if it was just a mysterious vanishing of the footprints.

I tried knocking on the tree in several different locations to see if it was hollow or if it was a portal that just happened to look like a tree. I had not noticed that the Unicorn had vanished until he reappeared with Sherlock who immediately offered a comment, "You won't get anywhere like that, you know. Haven't you learned anything from observing me in the field, Watson? The Unicorn said you requested my presence."

I quickly turned to find Sherlock standing next to the Unicorn gazing at the tree with a confident look on his face.

The Unicorn came to my aid by replying, "Don't be too hard on him, Sir Wizard, you would have been most proud of the way he outwitted the bridge keeper and secured our passage across the ravine.

Sherlock walked towards the tree, and gave me a light pat on the back, while answering. "Well, that is good to hear. There is still hope for you Watson. Now if you will excuse me, I will open the hidden door, and we can continue following their trail."

I looked at him with relief and surprise, as well as bit of incredulousness. "But how could you know where the hidden door is? You just got here. There is nothing obvious that I can see."

"That is because you have not read my monograph on *Detecting and Revealing Hidden Doorways, Entrances, Passages, and Access Points with an Emphasis on the Unseen but Obvious Locking Mechanisms.* It is quite straight forward actually. In fact I would say it is elementary."

And with that Sherlock walked up to the tree and pushed a small round spot in the bark on the trunk, at which point there was a clicking noise and surprisingly, a large section of it swung open like a door revealing a set of stairs heading down into the ground. Even more surprising was the appearance of a small white-bearded gnome at the top of stairs. He was wearing a tall, red pointed hat, blue trousers, and heavy black boots. I have to say he looked just like one of the garden gnome statues that have been appearing in front lawns and gardens around London since Sir Charles Isham brought back twenty-one of them from Germany. They have become quite the fashion. But I must say, back home they are just statues yet here, I had one standing before me that was very much alive.

The creature looked at both of us and crossly stated, "First of all, it's not polite to open someone's door unless you have been invited in, and second of all this is an oak tree, not an "L" "M" "N" Tree. That should be obvious to anyone. Those trees grow in the woods behind the old school house. They are very handy for making alphabet soup you know. I suppose you are following Morgan le Fay and the poet. They passed by here not too long ago and took the underground passage. She said that if anyone came following, I should point them to the wrong direction."

With that, the white-bearded Gnome pointed towards the East saying, "Over that way is the wrong direction. All right, now that I have pointed out the wrong direction, I suppose you are going to want to continue to follow them through my tree house in the correct direction. Do wipe your feet and try not to break anything on your way through. If you would like to stop in for a cup of hot spiced mead, I am sure the Missus would be delighted. We don't get many visitors. In fact, other than Morgan and her poet friend, you're the only visitors we have had in ages. Creatures walk past our tree day and night, but no one ever stops in."

"Maybe it is because your home looks just like a normal tree, and they do not realize that it is someone's dwelling," Sherlock suggested, adding, "How did Morgan le Fay know to pass through your home? And if you do not mind my asking, where does the underground passage lead to?"

The Gnome laughed in a voice that sounded like someone crumpling a sheet of paper and responded. "Lady Morgan knows everything about the Faerie Realm. She is its Guardian. Why she would point you off to the East is beyond me. Everyone knows the Dark Forest lies in that direction. It's not a pleasant place to visit. It just so happens that the back door of our home leads directly to the underground passage that bypasses the Dark Forest. It can be rather confusing though. It is quite a labyrinth. Are you sure you would not like a spot of nice hot spiced mead?"

Sherlock shook his head negatively and answered, "Thank you very much, but not at this time. We really must catch up to them. You mentioned that the underground passage is a labyrinth. Do you know the way through it?"

The Gnome's eyes brightened and he beamed with pride. "Do I know the way through it? I should hope so. I created it. I dug it out myself. I needed to find a way around the Dark Forest. The trees in there are not very friendly, and their beastly obnoxious branches kept stealing my hats. They had taken so many, I would have renamed it the 'Red Hat Forest,' but the Missus said it would only attract a group of ladies in red and purple hats, so I left it as is. I decided that I would dig a path under the forest to get around them. My sense of direction at first was not very accurate, which is why it turned out to be a bit of a maze. I eventually sorted it out, and completed the passage. And now I don't have to worry about losing any more hats."

"That sounds excellent!" I commented, thinking the trail would finally get easier. But then the gnome elaborated and dashed all hopes of that.

"Of course, the roots of the trees have a nasty sense of humor and like to trip travelers as they walk through the passages. In fact, if you stand in some sections too long, they will tie your boot strings together."

"Well then we will just have keep stop walking until we get to the exit," replied Sherlock. Please lead the way good sir. Time is of the essence."

"Follow me," the gnome replied and turned to enter the tree, "but do watch your step."

As we followed the gnome into the tree, I asked Sherlock what he had found out in the round table hall of Camelot. It turned out that Morgan herself was not using the secret chamber, but she had a devoted servant listening in and reporting to her. Sherlock had deduced exactly when the spy was present and had previously instructed King Arthur to make a statement of such urgency, that the spy would need to immediately report to Morgan. Merlin and Sir Lancelot were following the servant while Sherlock returned to me.

The entry into the tree and the passageway were just large enough for the Unicorn to accompany us, and the glow of its horn emitted a soft silvery light which illuminated our way.

"I must say," The gnome commented, "this is the first time I have had visitors in my tunnel, besides Lady Morgan and the old gentleman, I mean. She did not stop for refreshments either. Why are you surface folk always in a hurry, with no time to appreciate the journey? Do you know how long it took me to make this passageway?"

Sherlock looked at the intricately carved wooden panels lining the walls of the tunnel and replied. "Well, to answer that question, I would need to know the distance we will travel before we get to the exit. I can see that you put great effort into the finish work. Tell me how long it took you to carve each one of the panels, and how long the passage is, and I will tell you how long it took you to make the passage way."

The gnome's expression brightened, as he replied, "Verily? You can do that? Actually, the wall panels come already decorated. As long as I needed wall support panels, me thinks they should be attractive to behold. The view down here would be sorely lacking otherwise. Wouldn't you agree? I am curious. How long do you say it took me to make this? It is 800 paces in length, not counting the 400 paces in wrong turns I originally took."

Sherlock considered a moment and asked him, "Is the soil density the same throughout the entire passage? By 'pace,' do you mean the standard measurement that is equivalent to five feet, or do you mean paces of your stride that would be a tad smaller?"

The gnome frowned and kicked at a tree root that was trying to grab at his boots. "Like I said, the tree roots can be tricky down here, but they are nowhere near as bad as the branches. I always say, you need to get to the root of problem." He then laughed at his humor and went on, "I do mean standard surface folk paces, and the soil is indeed the same throughout the whole passage, soft earth with many pesky tree roots."

Sherlock paused a moment and then answered, "Well in that case, considering the density and composition of the ground, your height, the span of your arms, the length of your stride, the quantity of material that would have to be removed, and the wall support panels that would have to be brought down here, the placement of support beams, the occasional retrieving of your tools from the tree roots, lunch breaks, and holidays, I would say it took you three years, two months, and twenty two days."

The gnome stopped in his tracks, turned, and exclaimed, "How could you possibly know that? I did not even know that. The Missus told me how long the task had taken when I was finally finished. I was surprised. I had no idea it had taken that long, but she was keeping track."

Sherlock replied, "It is all simply a matter of observation and noting the finer details, just like before you take another step you should probably take care of your boots, which have been tied together by the tree roots while you were standing talking. You did caution us not to stop for very long."

"What?" the gnome exclaimed while looking downward to his feet. "Pesky tree roots!" he muttered as he untied his boot laces. "We should keep moving. I still don't see how you could have known that. Were you spying on me?"

The Unicorn piped in, "He has no need to do that, Sir Gnome. He can tell you everything about yourself from a brief glance and even more if he looks really closely at you. Why, he can even tell you what you had for dinner yesterday."

Again the gnome stopped in his tracks and exclaimed, "No! Truly and verily? I am not even sure what it was. The Missus said it was a surprise, and after I tasted it, I understood that it really was a surprise. I did not *want* to know, if you know what I mean. I did not tell her that though. I said it was creative and left it at that."

Sherlock smirked, turned to me, and commented. "It is probably a good thing he left it at that. I don't think he would want to have known."

Then he turned to the gnome and pointed out, "You need to untie your boot laces again. Have you considered boots without laces?"

The gnome exclaimed, "Vexing troublesome tree roots!" and again untied the laces and continued down the path. The remainder of the underground journey was mostly silent except for occasional grumblings from the gnome of "How could he have known that?" "How does he do that?"and more than one time, "Pesky tree roots!"

We had reached the end of the tunnel, and were exiting into daylight, when a woman's voice coldly stated, "Well gnome, what is this? I thought I told you to send them off in the wrong direction. Perhaps, I should turn you into a lawn statue. I understand they are very popular in the England your wizard friend comes from."

We looked up, and there before us was Morgan le Fay.

Chapter 12.

A Very Odd Metamorphosis, (But it did not affect Sherlock one bit.)

We all froze at the sound of the voice, and even the tree roots seemed to recoil back into the ground. The silence was profound and terrifying as we waited to see what was going to happen next. Finally, the gnome turned to me and whispered, "What exactly is a lawn statue?"

Morgan le Fay merely smiled and stared at us. She was very attractive; being slight of build with long, copper colored hair. She wore a forest green gown with a lighter cape the color of jade. Her emerald eyes were clear and cold and seemed to hide another more bewitching side of her beyond what was visible. She had dried flowers sewn into the edges of her cape, and the belt she wore was, in fact, a willow vine woven around her waist. Several crystals and small pouches hung from the belt and contained who knows what type of potion or magic.

The gnome turned to her, and exclaimed in a nervous and trembling voice, "I did exactly as you requested, oh great Lady in Green. I pointed them in the direction of the Dark Forest. Did you mean for them to actually go *into* the forest? No one goes in there anymore. If you had said to send them into the Dark Forest I most assuredly would have done so, but you specifically said to *point* them in the wrong direction."

"And I can assure you he truly did his best to point us in that direction, Lady le Fay," commented Sherlock, "but it was more than obvious that your footprints did not go any further into the forest. I would have seen them if they had. The only possible way you could have gone is through the underground passage. You do realize, of course, that I have been able to successfully track you all the way from Lord Tennyson's chambers. It is only a matter of time before we catch up to you."

Upon hearing what he had said, I turned to Holmes and asked, "What are you talking about, Sherlock? What do you mean before we catch up to her? She is standing there right outside the tunnel."

Sherlock pointed at the ground and replied, "What you heard and saw was simply a projected image of some type. If you look closely, you will see she is not casting a shadow."

I looked closer and saw that Sherlock was indeed correct. Morgan le Fay was not casting a shadow! She was an image similar to the scenes we had seen of Lord Tennyson, except when she spoke, we could hear her cold calculating voice.

"So you have, Sherlock Holmes, so you have. Your skills in observation and deduction are outstanding, and you have successfully met all of the challenges I have left for you. Let's see how well you can follow me when I do this!"

And as she finished speaking, she waved her hands in a peculiar manner and uttered a phrase in an arcane unintelligible tongue, and before our eyes, the lady in the image began to shrink and change form, her body condensing while at the same time, sprouting gossamer wings and delicate antenna. I could not believe what I was seeing. It was terrifying, yet transfixing. I could not avert my eyes. When her transformation was complete, she had become a very large bee!

"Did you see that Holmes?" I exclaimed. "I am going daft, or has she turned into a bee!"

"A *Megachilidea Pluto*, in fact. It is the largest species of Leaf Cutter bees, to be exact. Knowing their habits and nature as I do, she will be considerably easier to follow. You know I have actually written several monographs on *"Analyzing the Behavior and Travel Patterns of Bees, with a Focus on Large Cleptoparasites and their Nesting Traits Primarily Looking at the Queens."* I never imagined they would be useful here."

The Unicorn responded, "You truly do speak another form of English in the time you are from, but I believe what you mean is that you can still follow her in that form. You are aware that she can change forms and metamorphosize as she chooses. Merlin also has that ability. They had a duel once that involved transformations into so many different creatures, it was like a visit to the Zoological Gardens back in your London, except the creatures kept changing right before your eyes, and your Zoological Garden does not have any manticores, griffins, chimeras, or trolls. It wasn't something you want to watch right after eating lunch."

Sherlock nodded and watched as the large bee that had been Morgan le Fay flew off and the image grew nebulous and finally faded away.

"That is nice to know," he muttered as he dashed off from the tunnel entrance into the woods, stopping here and there to closely examine various leaves, branches, crevices in tree trunks, and fallen limbs. With the air of a lecturer, he commented, "Each one of these signs tells a detailed story, Watson. Bees are elementary to follow, if you know how to read them."

The Unicorn replied, "I understand what you are saying. It is simple for me to read the signs of magic in or having passed through an area. When Morgan le Fey is not in her human form, she leaves a certain aura or disturbance in the air. I can assure you, Sir Wizard, you are on the correct path. Only certain creatures like myself can sense magic, but you are without question the only one I have ever met that can follow a specific insect."

At that point, the gnome stopped and held up his hand saying, "Verily, it has been most pleasant meeting you all, but I do not want to be around when you do catch up to her. She can be quite formidable, and it is time I returned to my home." .

Sherlock and I replied that it was pleasant meeting him, thanked him for the directions through the underground passage, and wished him well. In a moment, he had disappeared back into the labyrinth, and the Unicorn and I were following Sherlock as he examined cut marks in leaves and observed aloud, "Did you know, Watson, that fossil record of the Megachilidea Bees date back to the Middle

Eocene era? They are truly fascinating creatures. In fact, I am thinking about taking up bee keeping when I retire. Not that I am planning to any time soon."

The Unicorn stopped in its tracks and, looking off to the left replied. "If by 'retire,' you mean ceasing your present occupation to pursue more enjoyable but less profitable activities, you may not get that opportunity. Look over there!"

Not far in the distance were several small, hairy, and odd looking creatures with sly expressions on their faces. They looked rather mischievous and unpredictable. They were uniformly dressed in grey tunics, brown trousers, and black boots.

"Those are Hobgoblins!" stated the Unicorn. "They are the less friendly, distant relatives of Brownies and are most fond of practical jokes when they not doing something even more unpleasant. They appear to be planning something devious."

The creatures were grinning, muttering and pointing at us while looking from where we stood towards a location several yards down the path.

"Those are certainly an unpleasant lot of blighters. What do you think they intend to do, Sherlock?" I asked.

"Based on their behavior and actions, I would say nothing. They have already set a trap, and they are waiting for us to blunder into it. We do not have time to play their games, so I suggest we deal with them quickly."

With that Sherlock removed from his pocket several of the biscuits left over from his mead dueling contest, took a bite out of one them commenting on how delicious it was, waved them in the direction of the hobgoblins, and then threw them further down the path in front of us. The creatures as one leaped forward on to the path to grab the food and were at once caught in large wooden cage that suddenly fell from the tree above.

Holmes turned to us and asked, "Shall we proceed? As I stated, we do not have time to waste." And with that he threw one more biscuit into the cage, nodded in their direction, and proceeded to continue down the path.

The Unicorn looked at me and observed; "Now I see from where you get your cleverness and indifference towards food. If we run into any more obstacles, we will not have any provisions left. Still that was handled rather well."

Chapter 13.

A Very Odd Meadow, (But most inviting indeed.)

We left the area with the hobgoblins happily devouring the biscuits and seemingly oblivious to the fact that they were the ones trapped in the cage. One of them even muttered a thank you for the food and offered an invitation to return if we had any more. He assured us they would most likely be there waiting for us.

Holmes offhandedly replied, "I would imagine you will be, since I am quite certain that you have not read my monograph on, "*A Basic Guide to Escaping from Traps, Cages, Pens, and Prisons, With an Emphasis on Makeshift Methodologies Due to Lack of Proper Tools.*" It could have been quite useful." And then he went on his way, once more making minute observations on the behavior of the Leaf Cutter Bee and the ease of following Morgan le Fey while she was in the form of a bee.

As we followed Sherlock down the path, I heard in the distance behind us one hobgoblin ask the other two if they had understood exactly what the wizard was saying. One of the others answered, in between bites on his biscuit, "I think the wizard said he doesn't believe we have any libraries here." Surprised by his answer, I turned to look back and saw the hobgoblin removing a scroll from his tunic. He opened it up, and shrugged his shoulders, saying, "I cannot imagine what he is talking about. It says right here, *A Basic Guide to Escaping from Traps, Cages, Pens...*" and his voice faded off into the distance.

The terrain gradually transformed from a forest into a wide rolling meadow that was bursting with multicolored flowers as well as buzzing with a multitude of bees. I looked at the scene and my hopes crashed as resoundingly as a knight in a full suit of armor falling off his horse. How was Sherlock going to be able to find one bee amongst hundreds? I looked at the Unicorn and asked, "Can you tell with your ability to sense magic which one might be her or which way she went?" He shook his head and said that she had certainly passed through the area, but had apparently returned several times and then left again several more times going in a multitude of different directions. Sherlock stopped at the edge of the meadow and studied it intently for some time. I took advantage of the opportunity and observed the area myself.

I must say that in spite of our urgent task to find Lord Tennyson, this attractive meadow was truly a paradise, and I enjoyed the moment to take it all in. The blossoms were colorful, fragrant, and bright, with an abundance of different blooms. I felt myself relaxing and not being as concerned with which insect might be Morgan le Fey. There was an overpowering scent of lilac and tea rose in the air, which was very soothing. There were low hills and hedges leading off in many directions with narrow pathways alongside the hedgerows. It looked very much like a meticulously cared for garden and as if it was purposefully laid out. After a moment of gazing at it all, I began to notice what looked like minute structures that blended perfectly into the surrounding vegetation and grounds. If one did not look closely, they could easily have been missed, as they were so naturally camouflaged. Although they were constructed of twigs, branches, bark, moss, leaves, and other natural materials, they were most certainly miniature houses.

I was about to exclaim, when Sherlock held up one finger to his lips to request silence. I did not know what to expect, so I said not a word and remained motionless. My eyes darted about in all directions, wondering what it was he anticipated, when a number of tiny, winged but human looking creatures began emerging from behind the flowers and shrubs as well as from within the Lilliputian dwellings. The tallest of them was less than ten inches in height. Their wings were varicolored, iridescent, and gossamer, and they were the most delicate and perfectly formed beings I had ever seen. They were the very picture of gentleness and beauty. I thought to myself they must be faeries or perhaps pixies. I certainly had never seen anything quite like them before.

Very slowly, so as not to frighten them, Sherlock removed from his pack the musical instrument and bow that he had received as a gift from the dragon earlier. He set it against his shoulder and began to play. The creatures were immediately drawn to him. It seemed as if they were glowing as they fluttered around us bobbing and drifting to the exquisite melody. Their dance was a hypnotic combination of music and motion unlike anything I had ever witnessed. Once again, in addition to Sherlock's music, I heard a haunting second melody that played harmony and counter-point to his. The ethereal song of

Pixy Music was once more accompanying him. The two lines of their duet wove around each other playfully cavorting as if in a folk dance, then slowly and gently caressing as two partners in a waltz. I could hear pure ecstasy in their music, and the result was captivating. I found myself wishing it would go on forever. I thought perhaps, here in this mystical meadow, Sherlock would finally meet Pixy Music, but sadly she did not appear.

After an interlude, Sherlock stopped playing and with one hand, made a wide sweeping gesture in a circle. He shrugged his shoulders while holding up his hands to indicate a question. It was then I realized what he was doing. He had gained their confidence by playing the mystical music, and in sign language, he asked them which way we should travel. How they could possibly know what direction we wanted to go or even that we were following Morgan le Fey was quite beyond me, but I knew better than to question the deductions of Sherlock Holmes.

The faeries must have understood him, however, because they fluttered in one direction heading towards the east and paused. They returned to him and repeated the motion. He bowed his head to the group in acknowledgement and replaced his makeshift violin and bow in his pack, then turned back towards me the Unicorn and gave a quick tilt of his head in the direction they had shown to indicate that we should again be on our way. He straightforwardly added, "We really must be off, Watson. There is no time to spare. We are not far behind Morgan le Fey and Lord Tennyson, and as I played, I felt the presence of Pixy Music. It was exquisite. I know she is not far away."

I must say I was reluctant to leave the charming meadow. I felt I could lie down and bask in the peace and serenity forever, but I knew we had to keep moving to find Lord Tennyson. Holmes was already leaving, so with considerable effort, I forced myself to keep going.

While Holmes was as observant and diligent as usual, he was somewhat quieter while he followed the trail, keeping his perceptions and deductions to himself. I am sure that he was reliving the delight of his musical interlude, as well as wishing Pixy Music had actually appeared. The Unicorn, however, was more vocal in its observations. "I must say, Dr. Watson, you did a champion job of resisting the temptations of the Faerie meadow. You are aware, of course, there have been many travelers to this mystical vale who have come here and never had the strength to leave."

I looked at the creature and suddenly realized how tempting the urge had been and I was very thankful that Sherlock had been so insistent.

The Unicorn nodded in Holmes' direction and added, "Should your wizard friend ever grow tired of following clues or bees, he would indeed make an excellent court musician. Of course, he will first have to successfully resolve his encounter with the enchanted Mirror that stands in our path."

Chapter 14.

A Very Odd Mirror, (And Sherlock proves there is most certainly more than one way to look at things.)

I looked up and saw not far along our path a large oval mirror mounted in a carved wooden frame set in the middle of the road. The wood work surrounding it was very ornate, detailed, and of the finest quality. It looked more like something that one would find in a palace, not sitting in the middle of a remote path in the wilderness. But then in this place one never knew what to expect.

Sherlock approached the mirror slowly while commenting, "Hmm, what have we here? It appears to be a fairly standard looking full-length, glass mirror, mercury backed, with beveled edges set in a carved mahogany frame with images of Camelot, King Arthur, and his knights on one side, while the other side featured Morgan le Fey and various faerie creatures. Most intriguing…

"The image is somewhat odd though. I can see myself, but the background appears to be rather blurred. It is almost as if the reflection is not certain or exact. How strange… Did you know, Watson, that there is a great deal of superstition and fear connected with mirrors? They are said to be able to capture one's soul, which is why household mirrors are typically covered with drapes at the time of a death in the family to prevent the soul of the dearly departed from being trapped inside it. Breaking a mirror is thought to bring seven years of misfortune, and some believe that mirrors can be a portal or doorway to other realms. I am sure Lewis Carroll could have told us a great deal about that.

"Alfred Lord Tennyson himself wrote a poem, *"The Lady of Chalot"*, in which the lady in question was cursed to view the world only through the reflections in a mirror. When she did dare to look directly at Camelot, the mirror cracked and she fell dead. Rather sad actually. If you had read my monograph, *"A Complete History and Analysis of Mirrors as They Relate to Problem Resolution, Clue Detection, and Crime Solving With an Emphasis on Determining the Unknown,"* you would certainly understand what I am referring to."

Just then a profound, crystal clear feminine voice resonated in the still air, seeming to come from nowhere and everywhere all at once. It surrounded us with a deepness that echoed like a bottomless pit, with tendrils that pulled you deeper and deeper into it no matter how much you resisted.

"That is an interesting and reflective, if somewhat superficial, discussion of mirrors, Sherlock Holmes; not surprising considering your purely observational and analytical approach to subjects. You have really only scratched the surface, if I say so myself, which, based on my personal experience as a mirror for the last 150 years, I do feel qualified to say so. You neglect to mention that mirrors can also show the past and the future, what has been, what may be, and what will be."

As the voice spoke, the image in the mirror began to change and no longer showed Sherlock's reflection, even though he was clearly standing in front of it. First the mirror showed Sherlock sitting in his chair across from the Cheshire Cat, followed by the Hatter and White Rabbit entering 221-B Baker Street. Then a hazy blur of images from the Grinning Cat Adventure appeared, followed by Captain Nemo of the *"Nautilus"* coming through our doorway and then a number of reflections from the *"Nautilus"* Adventure.

The image then grew dark and cloudy and showed a struggle between two men on cliff overlooking a waterfall. They each seemed very skilled and evenly matched with neither gaining the upper hand, when suddenly one of the two made a move that forced them both over the cliff and down into the falls. I felt a grip of terror overcome me when I saw the expression of one and realized that it was Sherlock Holmes himself. After that, the mirror grew black reflecting nothing at all, and the crystalline voice went on: "Mirrors can show your greatest desires, or your worst fears. They can show what you long to see more than anything in the world or what you would close your eyes forever not to behold. The greatest question, Sherlock Holmes, is what truly lies behind the mirror? Are you prepared to answer that question?"

I was still trembling in fear from what I had seen the Mirror foretelling of the future when Holmes replied, "What lies behind the mirror depends on the perspective of who is standing before the mirror. It depends on what they bring and what they seek to take away. It also depends very much on the inclination of the mirror itself. You should understand that better than anyone, Mirror. How many other false images have you reflected before today?"

"That is an astute observation, Sherlock Holmes. All of the false images that I have ever revealed were no more than what the person seeing it wanted to see or what they despaired more than anything, the very thought of seeing. It is not my fault that after seeing the image, they themselves caused it to happen."

Sherlock edged closer to the surface of the Mirror and responded, "Is it the fault of the arrow, the bow, the string, or the hand that releases the arrow from the bow which causes a death?" he asked. "Or could it be the fault of the creature that happens to be standing where the arrow strikes? When you reflect a death, are you drawing that person to its exact location at that time and therefore causing it to happen? Are you spinning a web of deceit? What is your perspective, Mirror?"

The Mirror's image changed from darkness to swirling grey clouds, and the voice grew angry. "No one dares to question the reflection in the Mirror! I can show you the very moment of your death, if I desire. And it will haunt you the rest of your life."

Sherlock calmly stood his ground and replied, "You can show me anything you desire, but if I do not accept it as reality, it means nothing to me."

The grey and black clouds in the Mirror's surface swirled more violently than ever. Lightning bolts flashed and illuminated the image. The entire surface of the Mirror seemed to be trembling and shaking in the frame.

"Nothing? Nothing you say? Behold this!"

The clouds in the Mirror parted, and the image returned to the scene of the waterfall that I had chanced a glimpse of earlier. "*NO*' I thought to myself, not that! But Sherlock did not seem to be concerned in the least.

"Each of us creates our own destiny," he proclaimed to the Mirror. "Each of us is in control of every situation in which we place ourselves."

At that point, the image in the Mirror seemed to flutter and change. There was a ray of sunlight that pierced the clouds, and in that light, I saw only one of the two figures fall to his doom. I could not see the face of either, but Sherlock was smiling as he stood defiantly before the Mirror.

"I do not choose to see what *you* would desire to show me but only what *I* would choose to see. Now show me what is behind the Mirror, what is beyond the Mirror. Show me where I will find Morgan le Fey and Alfred Lord Tennyson. Show me what she has done with Nimue, the Lady of the Lake!"

The Mirror was shuddering even more violently than before as the image showed Morgan and Lord Tennyson sitting calmly in front of the entrance to a cave located in a peaceful vale surrounded by lilacs and roses. In a nearby pool, which seemed to have some type of energy dome over it, Nimue, the Lady of the Lake, was trying to break the enclosure that held her prisoner. The lightning bolts in the Mirror again began flashing around the perimeter of the image clouding the picture. It seemed as if lightning was crackling on the very surface of the mirror itself. Sherlock, sensing that something was about to occur, reached beneath his robe. As a bolt of lightning arced from the Mirror directly towards him, he quickly removed and held up a small pocket mirror which reflected the lightening straight back towards the enchanted Mirror. All at once, there was a brilliant flash, accompanied by a deafening crash of thunder, and then all was silent. The surface of the Mirror was once again normal, if there is such a thing in that odd land. It simply reflected the image of Sherlock standing before the Mirror with the wooded background behind him. It looked no different than any other reflection.

Holmes turned towards us, sighed, and addressed the Unicorn asking, "Good creature, would you happen to know where in this uncanny land the cave near a pool surrounded by roses and lilacs might be found? We must be on our way to rescue not only Lord Tennyson but Nimue as well."

Chapter 15.

A Very Odd Discussion, (And Sherlock actually sees the invisible.)

The Unicorn replied, "We are going in the correct direction." And it returned to the pathway with Sherlock walking along next to the creature, observing the rocks, vegetation, and trees. I quickened my pace to catch up to him. Not knowing quite what to say, I commented, "Well, that was rather unusual, wouldn't you say, Holmes old boy?"

He turned to me and answered, "Watson, for all of the sensational exaggerations and over romanticizing in your accounts of my adventures, you sometimes have the most incredible gift of understatement imaginable. Seeing various possibilities of one's death portrayed by a vindictive enchanted Mirror is more than what I would call "unusual." It's somewhat like going for a Sunday stroll and seeing your gravestone, except without the friendly spirits of Christmas Past and Present and the happy ending that that Dickens fellow was writing about. It took all of my strength to reject her influence and create my own destiny. However, I will be a bit more cautious when it comes to waterfalls though and possibly in the bath as well."

"How can you be so cavalier about it all?" I asked adding, "But you did succeed, Holmes! You not only rejected her manipulations and suggestions, but now you know where Lord Tennyson and Nimue might be."

"What other attitude should I take, Watson? I am not going to avoid any running water I come across. That might end up inadvertently causing my own downfall, which in effect would end up fulfilling her prophesy of a waterfall being my downfall, either literally or figuratively."

The Unicorn then interrupted, "Dr. Watson, in observing your Wizard friend all this time, I am certain he would never fall for that. He is much too clever. I am more curious to know as to how we are going to find and get to the Island of Avalon where the cave is located."

"What did you say?" Sherlock and I both turned and asked at the same time. "Are you saying the cave is on an island? Where?" We asked in unison.

The Unicorn answered affirmatively, "What I said was, the cave that was shown in the mirror's image is on the Island of Avalon. Yes, it most definitely is an island and being a mystical island, no one knows exactly where it is except the three Faerie Queens: Morgan le Fe, the Guardian of the Faerie Realm, Nimue, the Lady of the Lake: and the other one."

"The other one?" I asked. "Who is the other one?"

The Unicorn turned its head to an angle, thought for a moment, and answered, "That is an interesting question. She is more mysterious, and less is known about her than the island itself. It has always been said that there are three Guardian Queens of Avalon, and we know she really does exist, but she has become such a recluse that no one really knows anymore who she is or where she can be found."

"What about Merlin?" I asked. "I would think he would know the answer or at least be able to figure it out. He is almost all knowing. After all, he found Sherlock Holmes centuries in the future. What is a simple mystical queen who wishes to remain hidden? How difficult could that be?"

"An excellent question, Watson", Sherlock answered. "That is, indeed, the question. And deducing the answer after careful observation is a job for the consulting detective, and fortunately for us, I happen to be the best one in this time period or any other. Unicorn, you recognized the image of the cave as being on the island of Avalon, yet you say that its location is unknown. How is that possible?"

The Unicorn stopped walking, looked up into the sky for a moment, and replied, "It was long before Arthur's time. It is said that the three Queens were Guardians of the mystical Island of Avalon. It was a place of healing and peace. When people were seriously sick or injured, they were taken there to be healed. Once they had recovered, they were returned to Faerie Land, or wherever it was they came from. Many of them described the beauty, magic, and enchantment of the place. They longed to return, but the island remained hidden. That is how I came to hear of it and how I recognized the description. The location in the Mirror's image was unmistakable.

"When Arthur came, there was a difference of opinion between Morgan and Nimue. As you already know, Nimue supported Arthur and what he was doing, while Morgan stood against him. The third queen, I believe her name may have been Aoleous, but no one knows for sure; she chose to remain neutral and simply vanished."

Sherlock seemed deep in thought as he nodded his head, "Yes! Of course she did. What else could she do? She needed to remain aware and accessible to the island but not in an obvious or open way, so she changed her identity and became someone else able to traverse multiple realms, to listen to and communicate with all of them, yet still be able to observe the Faerie Realm and Avalon, unseen and unknown. It all makes perfect sense. She has been hiding in plain sight, so to speak."

I stood dumbfounded not knowing what on earth he was talking about. "Holmes, I know you can see minute details of situations that no one else does and that you can put two and two together in ways that would equal any number you might need to fit your equation, but I have no idea what you are getting at. Could you please explain yourself?"

Sherlock was actually smiling as he whispered, "No, Watson, you would not, nor could you ever, but it is so obvious."

And with that he walked over to a medium-sized rock, sat down, took out his improvised violin and bow, set it to his chin, and began playing it.

The Unicorn looked at me with a puzzled expression and asked, "Does he do this kind of thing often? I mean make obscure and cryptic statements about a subject and then just sit down and start playing music?"

"You have no idea." I answered, adding, "Actually, yes, quite often. This is rather normal behavior for Sherlock Holmes."

Sherlock, however, was oblivious to our discussion. He was lost in his music, which was, once again, exquisitely beautiful. It was a haunting melody, which danced and played on the wind echoing, during brief moments of profound silence. I was certain I could hear the accompanying strains of Pixy Music's melody as well. They were interweaving and harmonizing, in addition to calling and answering each other musically. Sherlock would play a line of a deep tonal chords followed by Pixy Music answering with a light and delicate refrain. The result was multilayered and resonating with a musical depth and beauty beyond imagination.

I had stood for quite some time overwhelmed with fascination, and mesmerized by what I was hearing when I noticed that there seemed to be a radiant glow hovering in the air near where he was seated and playing his unworldly melody. The accompanying song that was Pixy Music's seemed to be emanating directly from within the glowing cloud. There appeared to be a form of some type inside the hazy aura, but I could not make it out. Could that be her, I wondered. Was she finally here? I was certain that this time he might actually meet her and realize his longing desire. The intensity of the music grew in energy and passion, reaching a quavering crescendo, but sadly that was all.

The glowing radiance gently faded away as the captivating music came to a halt and the last echoes evaporated into the air. I was waiting quietly for Holmes to say something, when the Unicorn broke the silence stating rather straight forwardly, "So it turns out that the missing third Queen of Avalon is Pixy Music. That explains where she disappeared to. As you said earlier, Wizard Holmes, it really does make perfect sense."

With his eyes closed, savoring the interlude they had shared, Sherlock sighed and responded, "I saw her, Watson. This time, I actually saw her."

Chapter 16.

A Very Odd Game of Chess, (And Sherlock clears the board, literally.)

With a far off expression, Sherlock sighed again, "This time, I really, truly saw her! Watson, she is beauty beyond description. She is incomparable! While her haunting music is unimaginably enchanting and captivating, it is a mere reflection of her physical grace and charm. If you were to gather all the delicate, majestic loveliness in the entire universe and all of creation and combine it into one form, it could not hold a candle to her. I shall never find another woman this attractive for the rest of my life. Perhaps someday, there may be a woman… one woman, that can possibly match me in knowledge, wits, or trickery and she will be known as *"the woman,"* but there will never be another for me."

I looked at him and asked, "Holmes, are you feeling alright? Not once before today have I ever heard you speak like this."

The Unicorn gazed at Holmes and stated, "It was said that the third Queen of Avalon was most stunning in appearance, but few beings are around who remember. Perhaps, like your wizard friend, they were so star struck, bewitched, and overwhelmed that they have forgotten the entire experience."

Holmes sighed again, shook himself all over, and went on, "Yes, I do understand. My heart longs to remain here communing with her forever but our task is calling. We need to continue on the trail. She did tell me where Avalon is located. And she also cautioned me that the situation may not be what it seems and to be careful in how I interpret things."

Turning to look at me, he shared, "She also said that you, Watson, have a considerable role to play in this game, and it will become more obvious before it is finished. Just do not jump to conclusions."

I looked at him with a puzzled expression wondering what exactly she meant by that. "What do you think she was saying, Holmes? After all, you are the detective and the one following the clues. That is your specialty. You are the one Merlin specifically requested. How would I make a difference? All I do is gather the details and record the adventure when it is all over. Anyway, you have successfully tracked Morgan le Fey and Lord Tennyson this far. Where do we go from here?"

With a stamp of one hoof, the Unicorn echoed my question, "Yes, where are we headed? With my swiftness, we could be there already."

"But forsooth, you cannot go anywhere, Sir Wizard," an elderly female voice creaked. "Your assistance is desperately needed here.

Alas, my son is trapped. You are the only one that can save him. Will you help a poor old woman?"

We turned and looked in the direction of the voice and saw an aged woman, leaning on a walking stick. She was dressed in typical peasant garb for the time period. Her wrinkled skin gave the appearance of considerable age. The long grey hair flowing down her shoulders still showed signs of once being reddish in color, but her green eyes were bright and alive looking. Sherlock addressed her asking, "What do mean he is trapped, gentle woman? Where might he be and who or what is trapping him? And why do you call me a wizard? I am only a mere traveler passing through these lands."

The old lady threw her head back and laughed. She raised her walking stick and pointed at me and the Unicorn answering, "One who travels in the company of a Unicorn and has an apprentice, and who can summon pixies with enchanted music. You may be very modest good wizard, but you are still a sorcerer. My son is trapped in a game."

"A game?" I blurted out. "How can he be trapped in a game?"

"My son was captured by Sir Robert, and he will not be released until his captor is beaten in a game of chess. Sir Robert commands his captives to be the playing pieces on a large chess board. He feeds them and provides shelter for them, but they cannot leave until he has been defeated. I am an old woman and have no one to take care of me without my son. Can you please help, good sir? Can you free him? It is not far out of your way."

I looked at Sherlock, and asked, "What do you make of this Holmes? Do you trust her?"

"Can we trust anything in this place?" he answered looking off into the distance. "It should not take me more than four moves to defeat Sir Robert. Let us take care of this, return the lady's son to her, and get back to our task."

Then turning to the woman he asked, "How far away is this Sir Robert, dear lady?"

"Oh thank you, Sir Wizard. Thank you! I will be eternally grateful to you. He is just over the hill. You will see the large chess board in the center of his garden. He commands his captive pieces to stand at attention all day, ready to begin a game at the drop of feather. He also keeps several geese on hand so he has feathers to drop whenever he begins a game. He is a strange one, Sir Robert is. But forsooth, please do not tell him I said that, or I shall end up on the chess board as well."

"You need not worry, dear lady. I will not say a word," Holmes replied. "Please lead the way."

We began following the old woman, and I asked Sherlock if any part of her story seemed odd, and he answered that everything about the whole place was more than odd. It defied rational thought and logic, but it was still the way things were here, and he would apply his skills in observation, deduction, and rational thought to see where it takes us. He stated that he planned to write a monograph on the subject when we concluded this business. He was thinking on calling it *"A Logical Step-by-Step Guide to Finding the Reality in Unreal and Non-Logical Situations Using Observational, Rational, and Deductive Thought Process."*

I nodded and stated that it could be handy considering our current situation.

We quickly reached the estate of Sir Robert, the odd chess master, and it was as the old woman had said: A stone manor house stood on a low hill. There was a large chess board constructed of black and white stone tiles in the center of a beautiful enclosed formal garden. Brightly colored blossoms adorned the pathway leading into the playing area. The chess pieces were various people of different ages each wearing a tunic with the symbol of the piece that they represented.

Sir Robert, attired all in black, sat in an ornate chair that resembled a throne on the far side of the board, and the pieces that he commanded wore black tunics, while the people on the near side all wore white tunics. To either side of Sir Robert stood a number of men-at-arms dressed in black chain mail and holding pole axes and cross bows. I would presume this was to prevent his captives from trying to escape.

Sir Robert, himself was of medium build and rather slender. He sported dark hair, somewhat unkempt, and he had an intense, wild look about him. His eyes darted back and forth trying to take in everything at once. When he saw our odd group approach, he stood and addressed us.

"Ah, is this a challenger perhaps? And one who travels in the company of a Unicorn, an apprentice, and a crone. I am impressed. Do you seek to try your skill in chess against me? To be the one who frees all of my captives? You do understand, I have never lost a match, and anyone who loses the game becomes a captive to be part of my reserve playing pieces."

The old woman, looking somewhat embarrassed, coughed and whispered, "Oh yes, I may have forgotten to mention that little condition. But I am certain that you need not be concerned. I listened as you communicated with the musical pixy that haunts your thoughts, and you are most gifted in many ways, Sir Wizard."

Sherlock ignored her and stepped up to the platform that overlooked his side of the board. Looking first to the left and then to the right, he began speaking to his opponent in a loud formal voice. "I do challenge you to a game of chess, Sir Robert. I am Sherlock Holmes, a great Wizard who has traveled from the future to free your captives. I am a master of logic and deduction and have never been defeated. I see beyond the visible, and I know your deepest inner thoughts. Even now you grow anxious. Let the game begin!"

And with that, Holmes called out, "King's pawn, two spaces forward," adding, "You are doomed Sir Robert. You should surrender now to avoid the defeat which is inevitable."

The person representing the King's pawn moved forward two squares and stopped.

Sir Robert sat down and said nothing beyond, "King's pawn two spaces forward," with his pawn repeating the movement. Sir Robert's eyes were darting in every direction, and he looked uncertain.

Sherlock immediately responded with, "King's Bishop to Queen's Bishop four, if you please."

The gentleman representing the bishop moved to the space indicated by Sherlock, as Holmes continued to address his opponent. "It is not too late, Sir Robert, to avoid the disgrace of losing so quickly. Look around you; do you want to lose in front of all of these people, your guards, and the famous scribe, Dr. Watson of Londonderry? Your defeat will be immortalized for all of history."

Realizing what Holmes was up to. I quickly spoke up to add to the distraction and confusion. "Yes, I am the famous scribe and bard who records the Wizard Sherlock's victories and exploits and tells them for all to hear. They are known throughout the land."

Sir Robert, looking nervous and uncertain, was somewhat reserved and called out, "Queen's pawn one space forward," And his Queen's pawn took one step forward into the next square.

Sherlock replied, "It is just as I expected; your end is near. Queen to King's Rook five. Watch the left side of the board, Sir Robert. Watch for what is invisible."

The tall lady wearing the white Queen's tunic crossed the board diagonally to the space indicated by Holmes.

With just a quick glance at the chessboard, his opponent jumped out of his chair and called out, "I know what you are doing, but it will not work. I see your Queen hiding there. King's Knight to King's Bishop three! Your Queen is in danger!"

The Knight walked to where he had been directed and stopped, shaking his head the entire time, as if he knew what was going to happen next.

Sherlock laughed, and replied, "Queen to King's Bishop Seven. Queen takes Pawn. Your King is in Checkmate! The game is over."

The White Queen gracefully crossed to King's Bishop Seven, tapped the pawn on the shoulder and took his place, and the young lad left the board.

Raising his arms, Holmes addressed the stunned people who had been the playing pieces, and said, "The game is over for good. You may all go home now. You are free."

In one motion, all the captives who had been the playing pieces began to tear off their tunics and throw them to the ground cheering Sherlock. As they left the chess board, Sir Robert stood silently starring at the scene in disbelief. He had lost and in the four moves that Holmes had predicted. It was brilliant.

I looked over to where the Unicorn and the old lady had been standing expecting to see the old woman reunited with her son, but she was nowhere to be seen. Where had she gone? I gazed into the crowd of people, but they were dispersing quickly, and soon the chess board was empty. As Holmes stepped down from the player's platform, I told him about the old lady disappearing and asked him if he had seen where she had gone off to.

He said that he had not, but he was not surprised. He had had his suspicions about her from the very beginning.

"Then why did you go along with her and this whole chess game challenge?" I replied. "What if your distraction ploy had failed and you had lost? What would we have done then?"

The Unicorn tilted its horn forward and piped in, "I could have spirited us away from here in an instant, or possibly even less if Dr. Watson did not strangle me while trying to hold to my neck on for dear life." Then looking at me he added, "I really have not had that many close calls with trees, Dr. Watson. You should not be overly concerned."

Sherlock ignored the Unicorn's comments and flatly stated, "I did not lose, Watson, I won, just as I had expected, and in the precise number of moves that I predicted. I had the entire scenario worked out in my head, as soon as we arrived. It played out exactly as I had planned. It was quite elementary. Regarding the old lady, I believe that this was all just a test of our character. And when she found out what she needed, she left."

"But who was she?" I asked.

"I am certain she is the very Morgan le Fey whom we have been following. It appears she has been following us as well."

Chapter 17.

A Very Odd Plan. (And possibly one of Sherlock's most outlandish.)

"What?" I exclaimed. "She was within our grasp the entire time, and you let her escape? What were you thinking? Why would you do that?"

"She did not threaten us in any way, Watson. She asked if we would go out of our way to help her, and we did. That told her something about us and our character. If you have noticed, besides the fact Alfred Lord Tennyson is missing, there has been no evidence that any harm has come to him."

"But what about the fact, that she is holding Nimue prisoner in the domed pond?" I replied "What about that? That does not seem very harmless."

He nodded and answered, "Well, yes, there is that. I do not have all of the answers yet, but I am getting closer, and I am sure there is more than what meets the eye."

"That is an understatement, Holmes," I replied.

"Indeed, Watson, but right now, I suggest we be on our way, as Sir Robert will not be very pleased with his loss, and we do not know what he may do next."

Neither of us was prepared for what did happen next, as Sir Robert, his men at arms, the chess board and gardens, and his entire estate vanished into thin air. One moment they were there, and the next they were gone, leaving a grey mist drifting over the hillside. We stood alone with the Unicorn on top of a barren low hill with only the solitary stairs and platform, that Holmes had directed his chess pieces from. Nothing else remained where the rest of the estate had been just a moment earlier.

I looked at Sherlock and said, "I do not know what you were thinking he might do, but this certainly is not what I would have expected."

The Unicorn looked around and added, "Sir Wizard, when you defeat someone in chess, I must say that you do not leave anything in doubt. There is no possible chance of a rematch here. None at all. Pray tell, how did you accomplish this?"

Holmes looked at us and answered, "It is as I thought; this entire experience was an illusion. The only things that were real were the stairs and platform that I climbed to play the game. You will recall that I never had to touch a chess piece to move any of them. I just called out the moves, and they happened. Or appeared to happen... I did climb the stairs to the platform, so they had to be real, but everything else was an illusion, a projected image. As I said Watson, this entire game was just a test."

I was perplexed. "Well then, is any of this real? Will all of Faerie Realm and Camelot disappear next? What exactly is going on here?"

"My belief is that Morgan le Fey has been observing everything we do and is evaluating us."

"But why?" I exclaimed. "What is the purpose of it all? If she had wanted to stop us permanently, it appears that she could have done so many times by now. After all, she was able to entrap the Lady of the Lake, and she is also a powerful enchantress. Most of the obstacles have been challenging to some degree, I will grant you that, but you have handled them all quite admirably."

"Watson, we will discover the answer to that when we bring this odd adventure to its conclusion, and to do that we must be on our way."

Then turning to the Unicorn he asked, "Would you happen to know the way to Somerset? That is our next destination."

The Unicorn's eyes brightened, and it nodded affirmatively answering, "Somerset, the location of Glastonbury! It is a very special place indeed. Of course I do. Every Unicorn worth its name knows the location of Somerset. I can have us there in an instant or perhaps two for your friend Dr. Watson."

"Excellent!" said Holmes, "If you can convey us there to a safe and not too visible location that would be excellent. Then, if you please, find Merlin and bring him to us as well."

I have to say I am not sure which was less appealing, slowly making our away along the trail and encountering who knew what kind of mystical creature, challenging obstacle, or deadly trap, or another ride on the back of a Unicorn at unheard of blinding speeds, narrowly missing trees and other potential obstacles. I did not have long to consider the question, though, as the Unicorn blurred, disappeared, reappeared beneath me, and we were off.

The wind whipped wildly past us as we wove our way through a forest of trees, stone monoliths, and other objects that seemed as if they were trying to jump directly into our pathway. I held my breath and secured my grip while closing my eyes as the Unicorn raced its way there.

We came to an abrupt stop, and the Unicorn calmly stated, "You can stop strangling me now, Dr. Watson, We have arrived."

I released my grip and found myself standing in a sheltered wooded glen not far from an abbey as the Unicorn vanished to go back for Sherlock. I had previously read that Glastonbury had historical connections with Joseph of Arimathea, the Holy Grail, and even King Arthur, but I never expected to actually be here at this time in history.

In 1191, the monks at the Glastonbury Abbey claimed to have found the graves of King Arthur and Guinevere, but historians felt that it was a pious forgery to build up the renown of the abbey and increase pilgrimages to the church. Another belief connected to the area is that Joseph of Arimathea brought many relics to the location including the Holy Grail, but again, it has never been conclusively proved.

Sherlock arrived next with the Unicorn heading back to retrieve Merlin, so I asked him what he expected to find here.

Taking in the surrounding scenery, Sherlock answered, "Pixy Music showed me where the Island of Avalon is located near this vicinity, and that is where the enchanted mirror showed Nimue and Lord Tennyson to be. I asked the Unicorn to retrieve Merlin, since he is the most adept in all of the arcane and unexplainable abilities that we have witnessed on this odd little adventure. It may prove very beneficial to have him present when we do catch up to them."

"When we do indeed

Nimue will be freed."

Merlin's voice proclaimed, as he appeared astride the Unicorn. He then slid to the ground standing beside it and went on.

"You are doing well,

as I did foretell."

Sherlock turned to Merlin and asked, "What did you discover following Morgan's servant? Where did she lead you to?"

Merlin put his hands together, fluttering them like a bird answering,

"To a cage, there she went,

then a raven off was sent,

with a message this I know.

The question is, where did it go?

Into the woods it did fly

Vanishing into the sky,

but pray tell do not fear.

Its destination is quite near.

Yes, it's true, not far from here
the raven landed very near.

The answer soon will be revealed

before the morning bells have pealed."

"That is encouraging," I responded, adding, "So what are we to do next?"

Sherlock stared silently into the drifting, curling mists that surrounded the area. Then as a shrewd smile crept across his face and an intense glow shown in his eyes, he said simply, "I have a plan."

We gathered round Sherlock to hear what he had to say. I had previously witnessed, and even taken part in many of the grand theatrical ploys he has used to confound and capture his foes, but what he proposed was beyond my wildest imagination and would end up resounding through history itself.

He looked around, as if to see if there were any creatures in the area that could over hear us, and began speaking in a whisper. "We know that Morgan le Fey has both Alfred Lord Tennyson and Nimue on the Island of Avalon. With her arcane skills and abilities, she would most likely be able to see our approach to the island no matter how cleverly disguised we are," he nodded towards Merlin, "or how incredibly quickly we got there," and he nodded towards the Unicorn. "We need to craft a plan that will unsuspectingly bring her to us where we can spring a trap that will contain her. Then we can safely rescue Lord Tennyson and Nimue."

"That is an excellent idea, Holmes," I ventured. "What did you have in mind? It would have to be something quite profound to draw her away from Avalon. Morgan knows we are on her trail, so she will be suspicious."

He looked at me and answered, "Yes she will be. That is why it has to be something so significant, so far-reaching and absolute, that she would not even think of staying away."

Then after a long theatrical pause, he stated clearly and coldly, "That is why King Arthur and Queen Guinevere must die."

"What?" I exclaimed. "What on earth are you thinking, Holmes?

"That is a rather novel approach, but perhaps a bit extreme, if you ask me." The Unicorn observed.

Merlin's eyes grew bright and he broke out into a wide smile,

"Very clever, clever indeed.

Her suspicions would be freed.

She will walk into our snare

When she hears the news so rare."

Holmes motioned for me to calm myself and went on, "Not literally, of course. It will be a grand ruse. Arthur and Guinevere will drink from their goblets, and then collapse at the table. Merlin will be summoned and pronounce them dead. They will be taken away, and at that time the Unicorn will substitute replacement bodies created by Merlin as he did with Alfred Lord Tennyson when he was passing away."

Sherlock paused a moment to let it sink in and continued, "The word will be sent out that the King and Queen have died, and all those who wish to view the bodies and pay their respects should come to Camelot. It is very near Glastonbury. She will not be able to resist, and we will be there waiting for her. She would not suspect a thing. Merlin can then create the same type of containment sphere that Morgan used to entrap Nimue. Once she is contained, we can go to Avalon and rescue them."

I considered what he was saying, and asked him, "Do you think she would be fooled by the replacement bodies? If she is a sorceress almost at the level of Merlin, I would think she could somehow be able to sense if Arthur and Guinevere are still alive and in hiding somewhere. I don't think there is anywhere in Camelot or the Faerie Realm that you could hide them without her knowing."

"That is a good point, Watson," he replied, "That is why we need to have the Unicorn bring them to London of our time and hide them in our lodgings at Baker Street."

"Where?" I exclaimed even more surprised than at his first suggestion.

"That is a very novel approach. As long as they are not subject to motion sickness, it could work quite well." The Unicorn replied thoughtfully.

Merlin again smiled broadly.

131

"Yea, verily, it is so.

To the future they must go.

From her vision they'll be free.

In the future she won't see."

I shook my head in wonder and asked, "You want to send the current King and Queen of Camelot to 1890's London? Just think of all the things that could go wrong. That sounds more like something from a comedic fictional novel that the American humorist, Samuel Clements, would write. Giving them knowledge from the future could end up changing the past."

Holmes answered me, "That is why they would have to stay inside our lodgings at 221-B Baker Street the entire time. The Unicorn would transport them there near instantaneously, and they would stay inside and out of sight. As long as they do not read any of my books or periodicals, they should be fine. I really doubt they would be able to read modern English anyway. Mrs. Hudson can fix them a nice meal of tea and kippers with toast and look after them. You know there is no finer host and cook in all of London than she. They will be fine."

"You are certainly right about Mrs. Hudson," I reflected. But should we send a letter of introduction along with Arthur and Guinevere? After all, how will she react to the King and Queen of Camelot showing up in our flat in 1890's London?"

The Unicorn stamped its hoof and interjected, "I am sure that arriving via Unicorn will be more than convincing enough. I need no letter of introduction."

Holmes nodded and agreed. "That is true, quite true. And Morgan will not be able to sense their presence anywhere in this time period, so she will believe them to be dead. It is the perfect plan."

Chapter. 18

A Very Odd Execution, (But certainly not literally speaking, and Mrs. Hudson sends her regards.)

We all agreed that the plan was the best approach to bringing Morgan le Fey out of hiding, as well as freeing Lord Tennyson and Nimue. It would also give us an opportunity to safely speak with Morgan in a more secure environment, and to possibly work out the differences between her and Arthur.

After conveying Merlin back to Camelot, where the wizard begin creating the duplicate bodies of Arthur and Guinevere, the Unicorn returned with King Arthur himself, so Sherlock could explain the plan in secret without anyone in Camelot listening in and discovering what was about to happen.

The Unicorn appeared and bowed regally to allow Arthur to dismount. As he stood before us and I looked upon him, I realized how the myth and legend that surrounded him may have come to be. Arthur was tall and solidly built. His flaxen hair and beard had a golden tinge to them and his eyes burned with fire. He was a vision of perfection. He wanted to lead England to what he thought was the best possible future. After dismounting, he straightened his crown, and rested one hand on the hilt of his sword, Excalibur. He was the very picture of everything that had been written about him.

The Unicorn spoke first and introduced us to him. "My King, may I introduce to you the far-seeing wizard from the future, Sherlock Holmes, and his associate Dr. Watson."

We nodded our heads to him, and he responded courteously in kind.

"As Merlin explained to you, sir, they are here to rescue your poet and bard, Sir Alfred Lord Tennyson, and they have overcome many challenges and obstacles set by Morgan le Fey."

"Yes, I have heard of your exploits since you have arrived. They are most impressive. Now pray tell, what is it you have in mind?"

Sherlock drew in close and quietly explained the entire plan to King Arthur. I had wondered what his reaction would be to Holmes' outrageous scheme. He listened intently without interrupting, and smiling nodded his head. He frowned at least once and laughed outright on several occasions. When Sherlock finally finished speaking, Arthur put forth his hand to Holmes, shook it and stated, "You are a brilliant strategist sir. Your plan of attack is well conceived and thought out. I would not want to oppose you on the field of battle. I agree with you entirely on this. I look forward to Alfred Lord Tennyson's safe return and to finally dealing with Morgan le Fey once and for all."

Holmes leaned in even closer and said a few words to Arthur that I could not hear, at which the King at first frowned quite sternly but then relaxed, and again nodded his head affirmatively. They shared a few additional words regarding when the plan should be executed, figuratively speaking that is, and how everything should take place.

I turned to the Unicorn and commented, "Sherlock Holmes and I have had some very strange and unusual adventures recently, but never did I imagine I would see him speaking with King Arthur of Camelot."

The creature responded, "I fully understand you, Dr. Watson, I never imagined I would see the King of Camelot and all of England speaking with a sorcerer from a future land of mechanical dragons and more."

The Unicorn returned King Arthur to Camelot with a promise to be back for us before everything was to begin. Merlin had earlier stated he was going to send new disguises for us to be able to blend in better with the citizens of the medieval city, but Holmes had assured him that it would not be required.

Sherlock reached under his robe and from somewhere retrieved several different items of stage makeup and alternate clothing, and after only a few moments, I would not have recognized either one of us.

"That is amazing Holmes," I observed, "You really have a gift at this."

"It is simply a matter of visual misdirection in facial features and attire when it comes to changing one's appearance, Watson. Just take what is, and turn it into what isn't. In my little monograph *"An Overview on the Art and Science of Disguises, Theatrical Makeup, and Altering One's Appearance With an Emphasis on Obfuscation, and Concealing the Obvious,"* you can read more about it. It is quite fascinating actually."

Then the Unicorn returned stating, "Your disguises are truly outstanding, Sir Wizard, but your manner of speaking would still give you away instantly if not sooner. When we arrive in Camelot, it is best that you keep your conversation to a minimum, or even better, do not say a word."

It was time to begin. Holmes and I were to be conveyed to Camelot by the Unicorn and then wait in the grand hall until the plan unfolded. The chamber was typically full of people bringing petitions, supplications, requests, gifts, and various invitations to the great King Arthur and his Queen. We were certain that no one would notice us in the crowd.

We arrived in Camelot, and it was the most magnificent city I had ever beheld. The towers were tall and stately. The walls were imposing but welcoming. It was clean and bright and resplendent. It was a city of dreams come true in the most impressive way imaginable. It was golden!

After depositing us, the Unicorn vanished and was preparing to substitute the replacement bodies for the King and Queen. Holmes and I were milling about with the crowd when a peasant approached me and asked, "Good sir, have I seen you in this court before? You look very much like the stranger I met who claimed to be a traveler from a distant place called Connecticut, located somewhere in Yankee

Land. His name was Hank Morgan. That is an odd name if you ask me."

I assured the stranger that I had never been to Camelot before and that my name was certainly not Hank Morgan, agreeing with him that it was a very odd name, but not as odd as 'Mark Twain'.

Just at that moment, a great commotion arose at the thrones of the King and Queen. They had raised their goblets in a toast, drank from them, and collapsed. A great cry burst forth from the crowd. People rushed about in all directions. The Knights of the Round Table gathered round their fallen leader and his Queen to protect and help them in whatever way possible, but it was clear they were not certain what to do.

"Merlin! Where is Merlin?" Sir Lancelot exclaimed above the noise.

"I am here.

Help is near.

Silence all

in this hall."

Merlin's voice echoed over the crowds.

Merlin suddenly appeared standing near the throne extending his arms upwards in a gesture commanding them to be still. Then signaling to the knights, he called for Arthur and Guinevere to be carried into the Kings private chambers, and for everyone to leave the room so he could examine them.

The citizens of Camelot were fearful and murmuring quietly. How could this possibly have happened? Who could have been responsible? What was to happen next? What was the fate of Arthur's Camelot? I looked at Holmes and nodded. So far, it was going exactly according to his plan.

After a considerable period of time, the door to the King's chambers opened, and Merlin entered the grand hall with a sad expression on his face. The room fell silent as they waited for his announcement.

He looked out at them and stated simply,

"It is as we feared and dread,

The great King Arthur and his Queen are dead."

He turned and spoke to Lancelot, and returned to the King's chambers.

As bells outside began to toll the sad news, Lancelot raised his voice to quiet the crowd and stated that the King and Queen's bodies would be returned to the hall shortly for the citizens of Camelot to pay their respects, and that Arthur and Guinevere would be buried late that afternoon. Messages of the tragedy that had befallen Camelot were being sent across the kingdom as he spoke, and the Knights of the Round Table had vowed that they would not rest until the guilty party was found and punished. Camelot would prevail.

Then I heard the Unicorn's voice coming from behind a nearby tapestry, "Mrs. Hudson sends her regards to the both of you. She is honored by her guests and most happy to receive them, but she wishes you would have given her more advance notice to straighten things up and look her best. After all how often does one entertain the King and Queen of Camelot?"

Chapter 19.

A Very Odd Turn of Events, (I would imagine Camelot never saw this one coming.)

I smiled at Mrs. Hudson's message and breathed a sigh of relief to hear that Arthur and Guinevere had safely arrived at Baker Street. I wondered, what they must be thinking of modern England. What did they think of tea and toast with kippers? It would certainly be a strange experience for them. For that matter, what must they think of Sherlock's flat, which is possibly by far the strangest place in all of London?

After a short period of waiting, the doors of the King's chambers opened, a trumpet was sounded to call for silence. The bodies of King Arthur and Queen Guinevere being carried upon palls of purple satin, accompanied by two columns of Knights of the Round Table were brought into the center of the grand hall. Leading the procession was Sir Lancelot doing his best to avoid weeping visibly. Accompanying the group was a fair haired young boy dressed in a commoners clothing who silently seated himself on the floor between the two bodies after they had been set in place for mourners to pay their respects. I had never seen the lad before, but there was something very familiar about his eyes. His face was nondescript and plain, but his eyes were both far away and deeply piercing at the same time. They had a clarity that reminded me of something or someone which I just could not place at that time.

Sir Lancelot then spoke to the hushed crowd. "People of Camelot, England's greatest King, Arthur Pendragon, and his beloved Queen Guinevere lie here before you. They have passed on from this life, but their vision of chivalry and justice for everyone is still alive. Let us all pay our respects to them at this sad and tragic time. And let us not forget the wonder of Camelot that King Arthur created with his unequalled strength and skill in battle. Let us not forget the matchless beauty his glorious Queen Guinevere graced us with. There was none fairer throughout the land, and her laughter was the sunshine that made flowers grow and coaxed the blossoms from the trees.

"As Arthur's Right Hand, his first knight, his greatest knight, his best friend, and as the Queen's own champion and escort in her travels, my heart grieves sorely. I share your sorrow a hundred times over. I loved them both dearly. But they are gone. Now let us, with our every breath, go forth to your fields and mills, to your farms and market places, on the streets and in your homes, in all that we do, let us keep King Arthur's glorious dream that is Camelot alive."

Even knowing as I did that Arthur and Guinevere were still alive, I could not help but be moved by Sir Lancelot's heartfelt words, and a tear crept into my eye. He paused as the crowd cheered and applauded his eulogy. One could see him struggling to maintain his composure.

"The King's counselor, Merlin the Enchanter, has already discovered who is responsible for this cowardly act, and is off and away in pursuit of the guilty ones now as I speak to you. As Camelot's greatest knight, I promise you, when he returns with them; they shall be brought to swift and final justice."

"But who shall lead us?" a voice cried out.

"Yes, who shall be our king?" another voice echoed.

"A king! A king!" the crowd took up the chant.

Sir Lancelot raised his sword aloft to quiet the group and assured them, "By the Sword of Lancelot, I promise you that will be determined soon. At this time let us in silence pay our respects to our great and beloved leader and his dear sweet Guinevere."

While the Round Table Knights organized the people into orderly lines to pass before their departed King and Queen, Sherlock and I watched the crowd carefully for any sign of Morgan le Fey. I wondered what Sir Lancelot had meant when he said that Merlin was off and away in pursuit of the assassin. According to Sherlock's plan, Merlin was supposed to be right here, right now, ready to capture Morgan when she appeared, but he was nowhere to be seen. Would he actually be gone now, when he was needed the most? If Morgan le

Fey did turn up, what would we do? We had no defense against someone of her skills or power. This was not some common street criminal or cut-purse of London that we were dealing with but one the most well-known and feared sorceresses of myth and legend: except in this place and time, she was very much alive, authentic, and very dangerous. Possibly even deadly.

I glanced nervously towards Holmes, but he said nothing. He only nodded back towards the direction of the line of mourners to indicate that I should keep watching and be diligent. All we could do is continue observing and see what became of this day.

Possibly an hour had passed when an elderly lady using a walking stick neared the front of the line. In the same manner that the mysterious young boy, sitting on the floor between Arthur and Guinevere still perplexed me, something about this odd, old woman was somehow familiar. At the very moment she approached them, it suddenly dawned on me. She was the elderly lady who had asked for Sherlock's help freeing her son from Sir Robert in the chess match! She was Morgan le Fey! She was here!

I glanced at Sherlock, trying desperately to get his attention, but he was already aware. He pointed directly at her, and in a loud, clear voice yelled out, "Morgan le Fey!"

Several things happened almost simultaneously, as the old woman blurred and slowly morphed into the younger version of herself, which we had seen in the projected image before she had turned into a bee. Then the young boy that had been sitting silent and motionless the entire time boldly stood up, pointing straight at her, and spoke in a rhyming, ancient language that sounded like Old Celtic. A shimmering, iridescent sphere of energy appeared and began to form itself around Morgan le Fe. With each word of the boy's incantation,

144

the luminous glowing tendrils weaving back and forth grew larger and stronger by the second. Like the tentacles of a nebulous ghostly octopus flowing in and out and all around her, they slowly coalesced into a globe of pure energy that securely entrapped her. At that point, while still maintaining his stance with his hands pointed at the sphere, the young boy began to grow and age rapidly. I watched in astonishment as in less than a minute he aged into a grey haired, bearded old man who was none other than Merlin the Enchanter himself.

Morgan le Fey was absolutely furious and with both arms outstretched wove her hands in a circular pattern while speaking in a language that sounded similar to that in which Merlin had cast his spell. The sphere shuddered and glistened as it resisted her magical attacks. I wondered whether or not Merlin's efforts would hold and feared what would happen if they did not. While Merlin stood his ground in front of her, Sherlock approached the two, removed his improvised violin and bow from beneath his robe, and calmly began playing. An ethereal, haunting refrain that I immediately recognized as Pixy Music, joined his, and the two of them harmonized and interwove melodiously as Merlin's sphere glowed brighter than possible. His energy globe positively radiated strength and security. Though it was near invisible, like a vague shimmering curtain, it was stronger than the very walls of Camelot. As he played, Sherlock spoke to Morgan calmly, "We mean you no harm, Lady Morgan. This sphere is only in place to prevent you from hurting anyone."

"I will show you harm!" She screamed as she turned, raised one hand, pointed it directly at Holmes and spoke once more in that ancient tongue. A bolt of lightning burst against the inner surface of the radiantly glowing globe, crackling loudly, but it held strong, and

Sherlock continued to play without flinching, even though he stood mere inches from its outer surface.

"As I was saying, we mean you no harm, as I truly believe you really do not mean to hurt us. You only wish to save and preserve the ancient realm of the Faerie Folk. That is a noble gesture."

She had been just about to cast another spell when she abruptly paused. She gazed at him curiously and intently. She studied him for what seemed like an eternity and finally asked, "What exactly do you mean, Wizard of Words? I observed how you cleverly used distracting utterance to defeat the chess master. Are you using the same tricks on me? Be aware! I can see though them, you know."

While maintaining his musical interlude, he responded, "If you can see through them, Lady Morgan, then you know that I am telling you the truth. You tested my character back on the hill, and I was willing to go out of my way and deviate from our path to aid a helpless old woman. My words during the chess match were my way of ending it quickly and painlessly, to return the captive son to an old woman and to allow us to resume our task of returning Lord Tennyson to King Arthur."

While he was speaking to her, I had noticed that the Unicorn had again disappeared but did not give it any thought. This part of Sherlock's plan had worked brilliantly! Morgan le Fey was captured and securely subdued in Merlin's spell of containment.

The Knights of the Round Table, however, had all at once drawn their swords, but in the resulting confusion and clamor of the crowd, they were not certain what to do or who to point them at. Arthur's knights had stepped back, and the people had scattered in all directions when they realized that it was Morgan le Fey and Merlin who were combating each other. However, when Holmes began playing his improvised violin, with Pixy Music accompanying him, and then Sherlock calmly and peaceably speaking to Morgan, and she actually responded to him in a civil way as well, they all stopped in surprise and listened.

"Yes," she replied, "you do show a most unique character, more understanding and considerate than my poor half-brother. You observe and see things more clearly than he ever did. It was not I that killed them, you know. In truth I am most saddened that he is gone."

Sherlock smiled and replied, "If that is true, Lady Morgan, then you will be pleased to learn that they are not, in fact, gone."

As he spoke, an incredibly bright, silver glow that could only have been the spiral horn of light of the Unicorn returning filled the chamber as King Arthur and Queen Guinevere, astride the majestic white creature, suddenly appeared on the raised platform in front of the thrones. The entire hall fell silent as they beheld their King and Queen alive and standing before them.

Then pandemonium broke out as the crowd began to cheer, "Arthur! Arthur! Long live King Arthur! Long live Queen Guinevere! Long live Camelot!"

Chapter 20

A Very Odd but Pleasing Change in Circumstances, (And we avoid the Lair of the Lake Dragon.)

Like everyone else, Morgan le Fey was astonished to see them returned alive and well. "Arthur, how is it possible, brother?" She asked. "I could not sense the spirit of you or your Queen still present anywhere in Camelot, or in the Faerie Realm. You were nowhere to be found. I was certain that you both had indeed passed away. I was truly saddened to hear the news. Yes, I have stood against you and vexed your efforts with Camelot, but it was only because you would not honor the ancient traditions of the Faerie Folk. And I was rather angry with Merlin, but I have gotten over that."

Arthur held up one hand to firmly but courteously interrupt the conversation. "Morgan my sister, pray tell, we will hold these words for a moment while two others of us who are most important to how this adventure comes to a conclusion, but are not with us here right now, are retrieved."

Then turning to Holmes and I, he asked, "Sherlock Holmes, may I once again call upon you and your associate, Dr. Watson, with the gracious assistance of this most noble Unicorn, to retrieve our missing comrades?"

Sherlock reluctantly stopped his playing and returned his improvised violin to the recesses of his robe responding, "It would be an honor, Your Majesty."

Although Holmes had stopped playing, the enchanting, haunting sounds of Pixy Music's melody still drifted and echoed through the chamber, filling everyone with a sense of serenity. I could tell that Sherlock, while pleased to assist the King in bringing this very odd adventure to a close, was saddened to end this harmonious interlude with Pixy Music. He had truly believed that he would actually meet her before this adventure was concluded. Now it seemed to be coming to an end, and it had not yet happened. Yes, together their song had helped Merlin capture and contain Morgan le Fey, but now it was time to retrieve Nimue and Lord Tennyson, and soon this adventure would be over. Would he never realize his heart's desire? I felt truly sorry for him.

The Unicorn then blurred and vanished from the raised platform and appeared next to Sherlock asking, "Shall we be off to the mystical Island of Avalon? I believe that Nimue and Sir Alfred Lord Tennyson are waiting there for us, and you, Sir Wizard, said that Pixy Music had shown you the way to Avalon. However, I must request that I carry only one of you at a time. Conveying both King Arthur and Guinevere together, was a very special and rare circumstance and not one that I would choose to repeat, especially considering the nature of the route we must take this time to safely travel there. I assure you, you will understand more fully after we arrive."

Holmes sighed and stated that the requested traveling accommodations were more than acceptable, and with that, he and the Unicorn blurred and disappeared. I wondered how we would free Nimue from the pond, as the enchanted Mirror's image had shown a similar sphere over her, but then I realized that if Morgan was trapped in a sphere herself, then perhaps the one that held Nimue would no longer be effective. I would find out soon enough, as the Unicorn materialized beneath me, and I wrapped my arms frantically around its neck. Everything surrounding me became a multi-hued kaleidoscope like blur of light, color, and objects flying by at less than a hair's-breadth away, with the Unicorn racing like a wind-born spirit through field and forest, over hills and valleys, and astonishingly enough, what seemed like, over the surface of the water as well. I closed my eyes and cringed.

We came to a stop near the cave entrance we had seen in the image shown to us by the magic Mirror, and the Unicorn turned its head to whisper in my ear, "You can stop strangling me, Dr. Watson. We are here and not impaled on any tree trunks. And yes, you did see correctly. I can indeed run across the very surface of the water as well. It is all a matter of moving fast enough. If I had slowed down in the slightest, we would be visiting the Lair of the Lake Dragon right now, instead of basking in the glory of Avalon, thanks to the incomparable speed and swiftness of the Unicorn."

I thought for a moment, and tried to imagine what visiting the Lair of the Lake Dragon might be like and decided that in truth, I did not want to imagine it, much less visit such a foreboding sounding place. Instead, I gazed wide eyed in awe at the island that surrounded us. The Unicorn's brief description of "the glory of Avalon" was an understatement. The island seemed to capture all of the mystical enchantment and tranquility of the Faerie Realm, as well as the promise, wonder and magnificence that was Camelot, but in a way that was far greater than both of them combined could ever hope to be. There was a sense of peace and serenity that permeated the very air we breathed. The soft fragrant scent of lilacs danced sweetly in the background, while a delicate wisp of rose played hide and seek. There was no strife or danger here, just an overwhelming sense of eternal endless calm. I understood why Avalon was considered a holy place, a place of rest and healing. I realized why anyone who had ever been there would never want to leave. It was far beyond what mere words could possibly describe.

I looked towards the cave entrance and there sat Alfred Lord Tennyson, England's greatest poet, and Nimue, the mystical Lady of the Lake, calmly engaged in a conversation with Sherlock. I had been correct in thinking that with Morgan subdued, she could not continue to hold Nimue prisoner. In truth, it had appeared that before we left Camelot, her animosity had subsided considerably. Perhaps this entire conflict between her and Arthur would be resolved. Nimue was no longer confined in the pool and appeared to be unharmed and in good health.

Alfred Lord Tennyson also seemed to be well. His greying dark beard and long hair looked no different than in the last photograph I had seen of him taken just before he was spirited away to Camelot at the time that he had supposedly passed away. He did appear rather tired and haggard, probably as a result of his recent travels, but it was still as if he had not aged at all.

Holmes had introduced ourselves and very briefly explained to both of them everything that had transpired and that we were there to safely return them to Camelot where Merlin and King Arthur were waiting for them and anxiously looking forward to their arrival. He also assured them that Morgan le Fey was no longer a danger to them. Nimue sighed in obvious relief and thanked Sherlock profusely saying she would be most happy to be reunited with Merlin, but Lord Tennyson seemed somewhat quite and withdrawn. All he said in response was, "Well then, let us be on our way... All things must pass."

As we prepared to return and explained to them that the Unicorn would quickly convey each of us back to Camelot individually, the strangest and most wonderful thing occurred. The ethereal enchanting sound of Pixy Music began to emanate faintly from inside the cave. It was almost a whisper at first but gradually increased in volume until it was unmistakable. There was no question at all. It was without a doubt the very song I had first heard in Wonderland, then again on board the Nautilus, and yet again several times here in Camelot when Sherlock played his improvised violin. It was the mesmerizing and melodious song of the third Guardian Queen of Avalon, Pixy Music.

Sherlock stood entranced at the sound of it. He had not been playing his makeshift violin at the time it began, so I am certain it had come as a surprise to both of us. In addition to the celestial music, a golden warm and glowing light began to emanate from within the cave. I had no idea what to do, but Holmes, surrendering unequivocally, as if in a trance slowly walked towards the cave entrance. As he neared the opening, I looked further into the cavern, and it was there that I too finally saw her.

She sat upon a finely carved chair in the center of a dazzling array of quartz crystals that covered the surface of the cave walls and ceiling reflecting a rainbow of shimmering light. Two furry wolves, a reddish brown coyote with amber colored eyes, some large grey geese, and a few other smaller wild creatures were curled up together, peacefully resting on the ground surrounding her.

As Holmes had stated previously, her exquisiteness was beyond description. I will attempt to elucidate her appearance, although I am certain that words will most assuredly fail me. Dressed in the most delicate of fine lilac colored lace, she was playing a harp of varnished cherry wood. Her graceful fingers lightly danced upon the strings creating the most exquisite music. There were daisies woven into her long dark hair. Bright, sparkling hazel eyes were her most captivating feature. They were a deep crystal pool of liquid aquamarine. One could dive into and lose themselves in her eyes forever. If her eyes were captivating, then her smile was beguiling and tempting. One felt all sense of hesitation or reserve melt away, and one wanted nothing more than to remain endlessly in her presence for all eternity. Now at last I understood why Sherlock had said that for him, there could be no other, why he was so utterly mesmerized by her.

She stopped playing the harp and beckoned him to come closer to her. He drew nearer and stood in total silence. The wild creatures paid no attention to him except perhaps the coyote that raised its head, yawned, and then rested it directly upon Holmes' foot. I only heard a portion of their conversation, and it was heartbreaking. As a Guardian Queen of Avalon she could not leave this mystical land. She was a part of it, and the island was also one with her. A common spirit dwelled within both of them. She could continue to communicate across worlds and realms, and share musical interludes with Sherlock, but she could never leave. And similarly, she would not ask Sherlock

Holmes to give up his life in London of our era. He had done a brilliant job of finding Lord Tennyson, rescuing Nimue and even resolving the conflict between Arthur and Morgan le Fey, but it was not yet his time to be here in Avalon. It is foretold that there is much he has to complete in his London before he could again grace the shores of the mystical isle. He has a great destiny before him, and he must return to it.

They continued speaking softly for an interval, gently reaching out and clasping both of their hands together, embracing warmly, and then she vanished taking the iridescent light with her. The geese other smaller creatures had followed her to wherever she had gone, but the two wolves and coyote remained behind undisturbed. Holmes looked down at the resting coyote who was apparently quite comfortable and seemed to have no intention of removing its head from atop of Sherlock's shoe. Holmes turned to me, sighed and said, "Watson, it is time we went home."

Chapter 21.

A Very Odd Round Table Gathering, (And we slightly alter the path of history.)

I will spare the reader the vivid details of yet another high speed Unicorn ride, as someone may be reading this after a meal. Suffice it to say, we did arrive safely back in Camelot in less than an instant, and I do recall hearing Sherlock commenting, "That was most invigorating."

Alfred Lord Tennyson's opinion was, "Remarkable, simply remarkable! I must capture this experience in a poem."

Nimue observed. "That was beautiful! What a breathtaking experience. I had no idea Unicorns were as swift as the wind. When can we do this again?"

My personal comments on arrival are really not important, but the Unicorn replied that while it may have been rather close, we did not actually hit the tree.

I will mention to those interested, that if there is any measurable dimension less than a hair's-breadth, which, if you would like to know, is defined as an infinitesimally small distance, it was considerably less than that.

When we were all present, the first thing I noticed is that Morgan le Fey was no longer restrained in the energy sphere but was standing calmly and talking to King Arthur and Merlin.

The second thing I observed is that Merlin was no longer speaking in rhyme. I pointed out both observations to Holmes, and his response was most typical. "Well, of course, Watson, I would have been very surprised had it not been the case. We needed to create an event that would break their barriers and bring them together to speak to each other. There is no real evil in either of them. I saw that in all of the obstacles she placed before us. We were never in any great danger from any one of them. They were actually rather creative, if I do say so. I was thinking of compiling her challenges and adding some of my own creative skill and character tests into a short paper, and calling it. *"A Straight Forward Guide to Developing Challenging Tests of Skill, Character, Practical Thought Process, and Fortitude With an Emphasis on Dealing with the Logically Impossible, but Nevertheless, Still Right There in Front of You."* The title may still need some modification though. I will have to work on that."

He paused to reflectively consider the future monograph and then continued speaking. "Regarding Merlin's speech returning to normal, it is quite obvious. If you recall Morgan mentioned that she was angry at him, but she is over that now."

"But what does that have to do with his rhyming?" I asked.

"Do you remember the Unicorn mentioned that in her anger and jealousy, Morgan le Fey had put an enchantment on him to prevent him from speaking to Nimue? Merlin of course found a way around it by speaking in rhyme, something about the heart of a poet and love. Since she no longer desires Merlin and is over her anger, there is no further reason for her to keep the enchantment on him."

Wondering aloud I asked, "Who do you think she is in love with now?"

Sherlock looked at me incredulously and replied, "Really Watson. It should be obvious. It is not so much love, as it is a common, deep shared connection to Camelot and the Faerie Realm. Two hearts beating as one to keep both realms alive. Her new desire is Sir Alfred Lord Tennyson."

"What?" I exclaimed. "He is..."

"Yes, I know. He is old. So was Merlin, and he was her mentor, teacher and guide." He interrupted. "He awoke in her a love for the Faerie Realm. It is not surprising she had feelings for him. She eventually learned everything she could from Merlin and also realized Merlin and Nimue share a different kind of love, so now she desires another with a meaningful association to Camelot. There is no one other than Alfred Lord Tennyson that is so connected to Camelot and now the Fairie Realm. That is why he was so quiet and reserved when we mentioned that there was no further concern or fear regarding

Morgan le Fey. It should be obvious that he shares her feelings as well."

I was about to reply when King Arthur signaled us to follow him into the royal hall where the Round Table was located. I waited with my comment and entered the great hall with the rest of our companions. The Knights of the Round Table trooped in behind us and dispersed to their seats. The room was large but not overly so. Colorful tapestries depicting many different scenes decorated the walls with swords, shields, and other medieval weapons mounted on plaques in between them. The famous Round Table of Camelot took up most of the floor space in the room, and it was an emotional experience to behold a representation of such power and legend. The mood was much more joyous and celebratory than earlier. And when we were all settled, Arthur began to speak. "Friends, I thank you for joining me here at the Round Table of Camelot. We have gathered here many times around this symbol of unity and equality among my knights, but I was blind not to realize that my vision should apply to other creatures as well. I have learned much this day, and I want to share it with you."

Morgan Le Fey then began to speak and echoed his sentiment. "I too have realized a great deal and have come to terms with my half-brother. In the past, I stood against Arthur because he did not accept the importance of the Faerie Folk. He felt that the world was changing, and he wanted to bring Camelot and England into this new world excluding the realm of the Faerie."

"That is true." continued Arthur. "I did not believe that there was a place for magic, or the Faerie Folk, but today I discovered otherwise. Sherlock Holmes, crafted a plan to convince everyone in the realm I had passed away in order to bring my half-sister Morgan out of hiding."

I leaned over to Holmes and asked, "Is that before or after she tried to kill you with a lightning bolt?" but he ignored me.

"But to convince her that I was dead, I could not be anywhere in Camelot as she is able to sense my presence with her arcane skills. Wizard Holmes made it possible for me to visit the land and time that he hails from. It is an entirely different world than Camelot. What I saw in the brief time I was there showed me that it is a sadder place, a less golden place. It is place with no mystical creatures, no Faerie Folk, no magic at all. If that time is coming and that is what the world eventually becomes, we may not be able to stop it. But while I still draw breath, the Faerie Folk will be a part of Camelot."

He extended a hand to Morgan le Fey which she graciously received, and they shook hands. Their conflict had ended.

Morgan then resumed speaking and pointed at me. "I too had crafted a grand and multi-layered plan which involved you the scribe, Dr. Watson. While I am not as gifted in seeing the future as Merlin, I did discover that, as his scribe, you collect and record the exploits of your Wizard friend. Your ballads and stories are shared throughout your world, just as the great bard and poet Sir Tennyson's tales of King Arthur and Camelot are widely shared in your time. My plan was to bring the Wizard and you here so you could see, experience firsthand, and record the wonder and splendor of the Faerie Realm and the Faerie Folk before we all vanish. Then history will be aware of us, and understand that we really did exist. Each of your little adventures led to another, each sharing a different part of this magical realm. That is why Sir Tennyson agreed to come with me. The poet is so important to Arthur and Camelot that Merlin would defy time itself to bring the great Sherlock Holmes and his scribe to Camelot to find him. Your story of this adventure, Dr. Watson, will keep us alive long after Camelot is gone."

I did not know what to say. The entire disappearance of Sir Alfred Lord Tennyson was simply a ruse to get me here to witness and record the Faerie Realm before it vanished. Sherlock was just the key to making it happen.

Holmes leaned over to me and stated, "I told you that you had an important role in this game."

I was dumbfounded. Never before had one of our adventures turned out like this. I could not imagine what would happen next. King Arthur then stood up and answered that question and also altered the course of history for several hundred years.

"Friends, as a part of the Wizard's plan, my counselor, Merlin the Enchanter, created replacement bodies for my Queen and I to convince you that we indeed had passed away today. I am sorry for the grief it caused you, my loyal knights, but it was necessary. Now that you are aware of the truth and of the new life of Camelot, I declare that we shall bury these duplicate bodies. The old Arthur has died. Let him be buried and let there be new life. We shall bury them south of the Lady Chapel near the Abbey Church."

I nearly choked when I heard that and whispered to Sherlock, "Holmes, do you realize that Arthur is placing the duplicate bodies exactly where the Glastonbury monks will find them in 1191? For several hundred years, this was believed to be the very resting place of King Arthur and Guinevere. It was centuries later that historians declared the bodies to be a hoax. Your little scheme to capture Morgan is echoing loudly through history."

Holmes waved his hand dismissively and answered, "Yes, yes, and you are going to record and publish as truth a Sherlock Holmes adventure with Pixies, Gnomes, Dragons, a Unicorn, Merlin, Morgan le Fey, The Lady of the Lake, Guinevere, and King Arthur himself. Tell me Watson, is there any real difference?"

Chapter 22.

A Very Odd Conclusion, (And believe it or not, Sherlock gets outwitted by a Unicorn.)

This was almost more than even I could believe and having accompanied Sherlock Holmes in so many adventures, I have witnessed a vast amount of the strange and unusual. Yet there I was sitting at the legendary Round Table of Camelot with King Arthur and Guinevere. The infamous Morgan le Fey was pleasantly sitting close to England's former Poet Laureate, Sir Alfred Lord Tennyson. Merlin was gazing starry eyed at Nimue, the Lady of the Lake, and all of this had come about because one of the most well known sorceresses of myth and legend wanted me to witness and record it all.

Sherlock leaned over to me again and whispered, "I promise you Watson, you will never publish this adventure while I am still alive. You know my feelings on magic and the unexplainable. I have a reputation to uphold. If you print this, we will have a whole host of literary characters knocking on our door. We could have Dracula show up looking for Bram Stoker, and Frankenstein, his monster, or both of them looking for Mary Shelly. We could even end up with Dorian Grey looking for that Oscar Wilde fellow, and who knows how that would turn out."

I looked at him and realizing he was right agreed. "You are probably correct, Holmes. Not to mention what patient would ever visit a doctor who believes Faerie Land is real?"

The Unicorn who had been standing behind us interrupted, "I don't know about that, Dr. Watson. It could do wonders for you to bring in children and younger patients. It could possibly even increase your business. If you painted scenes of the Faerie Realm on the wall of your office you might become known as 'The Unicorn Doctor.' Not that Unicorns ever need doctoring. We just focus our energy inwards and heal ourselves. Any Unicorn worthy of its name can do that."

Sherlock turned and faced the Unicorn saying, "That is the second time you have used the expression, 'Any Unicorn worthy of its name,' yet during this entire adventure, you have never once mentioned *your* name. Why is that?"

The creature reflected quietly for a brief period and then answered, "You are most observant, Sir Wizard. I am on a quest, and I have vowed never again to utter my name until it is successfully completed."

"Really?" I responded. "May I ask, what is the nature of your quest?"

The Unicorn gazed into the distance. "Everyone knows the story of *"The Last Unicorn."* Every Unicorn worthy of its name can recite it by memory. It is actually quite well know in your own world, and I am certain it will someday be written down. I am trying to learn the secret story of the very first of my kind, *"The First Unicorn."* No one has ever discovered it, and it has remained the greatest unsolved mystery of all time. It would be a significant challenge even for you, Sir Wizard."

Sherlock considered the creature's statement and replied scoffing, "I am not so certain about that. There is very little that, with my skills in observation and deduction, I cannot perceive. Why I could most likely solve your little puzzle in my spare time between cases, if I so desired."

The Unicorn's expression warmed considerably and even its horn was glowing brighter. "I sincerely thank you! That is most kind and generous of you, Sir Wizard. It has been a great honor to accompany you and assist in your quest to rescue Lord Tennyson, and help you resolve the matter between King Arthur and Morgan le Fey. It will be even more of an honor to have your assistance in my quest. Now I am certain the mystery will be solved. I must go and tell Sir Percival that I may be away for an extended period of time."

The Unicorn happily cantered off in search of Sir Percival, and I looked at Sherlock while shaking my head. "Holmes! Did the smartest detective of all time and one of the most intelligent and logical people I have ever met just get talked into assisting an imaginary, nonexistent, mystical, creature solve the secret lost mystery behind the first of its kind? What a great adventure story that will make!

"Sherlock Holmes and the Mystery of the First Unicorn!" I can see it now."

Holmes said nothing except, "Watson, do not even think of it. I did preface my offer with; I could solve it in my spare time *between* cases."

I frowned and said, "Yes you did, Holmes. You certainly did. I imagine we will be quite busy with other cases when we are back in London. I am sure the Unicorn will understand. After all, the swiftness of the creature was only a small part of your success."

Sherlock gave me a somewhat incredulous look and replied, "Watson, you have learned more clever trickery from me than you have let on. Okay, *"The Mystery of the First Unicorn"* it is." And he walked off muttering under his breath.

My attention turned back to the ongoing proceedings. I saw that all was still going well. Arthur, Lancelot, and Guinevere were conversing with Merlin and Nimue on burial arrangements for the duplicate bodies, while Morgan and Lord Tennyson were deep in conversation on the true symbolic meaning of Camelot as it pertained to the society of Victorian England and how she could not possibly fathom the significance unless she witnessed it for herself.

The idea of bringing Morgan le Fey to modern day England was inconceivable to me, and I shuddered at the thought of it.

I focused on the other conversation to hear Guinevere saying that a grand procession would be fitting, while Arthur said that a simple burial just placing the bodies in an oak trunk with a lead cross to identify them would be sufficient.

Merlin stood up and stated that he would inscribe the cross in Latin with the proclamation: "Hic jacet sepultus inclitus Rex Arthurus in insula Avalonia," meaning "Here lies interred the famous King Arthur on the Isle of Avalon."

Nimue pointed out that the bodies were not actually being buried on the Isle of Avalon, and he may want to reconsider. Merlin simply replied, "Satis." Which I believe is Latin for "Close enough!"

He gently took Nimue's hand and the two of them left the room to take care of the arrangements.

King Arthur called Sherlock and me back together, approached us, and thanked us profusely for our help in finding and returning Lord Tennyson. He was even more appreciative to Sherlock for having made it possible for Morgan le Fey and Arthur to resolve their differences.

He did want to let us know that while our England seemed like a much sadder and empty place, Mrs. Hudson had been the perfect host and that she was just delightful. Almost whispering, he also mentioned that if we ever, for any reason, returned to Camelot, could we please bring along with us a good supply of Mrs. Hudson's Earl Grey Tea? He would reward us richly. After trying it while he was there, he had been saddened to learn that tea would not be brought to England for several hundred years. He promised us that if we did bring a quantity back with us it would remain a solemn secret, as King Arthur would never even think of doing something that could alter the course of history.

Holmes and I looked at each other and smiled.

The Unicorn reappeared and asked if we were ready to begin our journey, as we had to first make our way to Stonehenge, then through

166

the portal, and finally back to Baker Street. We said that at last we were, and we fondly bid our farewells to everyone.

Nimue thanked us again for freeing her and reuniting her with Merlin. Morgan also expressed her gratitude, and stated that should Sherlock ever want to play a really challenging game of chess, she was always ready and could easily checkmate Sherlock in less than four moves.

Holmes replied, "The only way that could ever happen is if I was asleep, and even then it would be difficult if not impossible."

In addition, Morgan stated that she was looking forward to reading my account of our brief visit to the Faerie Realm.

"I cannot wait to see "*Sherlock Holmes and the Round Table Adventure*" in print" she stated.

Holmes leaned close to me and whispered, "She has a better chance of beating me in chess than that happening in my life time."

As we were about to leave, a faint echo of Pixy Music's haunting, ethereal melody whispered softly nearby. Sherlock closed his eyes, breathed in deeply, exhaled slowly, and said, "Farewell my dear Pixy Music."

And we were off.

Chapter 23.

A Very Odd Return, (But actually not that surprising when you think about it.

We made it safely back through the Stonehenge portal and to 221-B Baker Street without any overly terrifying near misses; that is, beyond the normal ones that are a part of traveling via Unicorn. It was good to be home again in our familiar lodgings, but the clattering noise and pervasive smells of London seemed odd after the calm serenity of Camelot and the Faerie Realm.

When we arrived outside our flat, Homes asked if, as we had passed by the concert hall, I had noticed the advertisement for the classical music performance that was scheduled for that evening. I responded, "No. What is being performed? Anything interesting?"

With a cheeky grin, Sherlock answered, *"The Sorcerer's Apprentice."* Would you care to attend?"

I ignored him and did not say a word.

I did notice one slightly odd change though. The outside door of 221-B Baker Street had a new sign affixed to it. In bold letters it read:

"Mrs. Hudson's Lodgings

Recommended by Royalty."

And in smaller print beneath:

"Unicorns Welcome!!"

And in even smaller print beneath that:

"Please wipe your feet!"

The Unicorn turned to Sherlock and said, "Well, my dear Sir Wizard, we have safely returned from Camelot to your lodgings. When do we begin?"

Also from MX Publishing

MX Publishing is the world's largest specialist Sherlock Holmes publisher, with over a hundred titles and fifty authors creating the latest in Sherlock Holmes fiction and non-fiction.

From traditional short stories and novels to travel guides and quiz books, MX Publishing cater for all Holmes fans.

The collection includes leading titles such as _Benedict Cumberbatch In Transition_ and _The Norwood Author_ which won the 2011 Howlett Award (Sherlock Holmes Book of the Year).

MX Publishing also has one of the largest communities of Holmes fans on Facebook with regular contributions from dozens of authors.

www.mxpublishing.com

Also from Joseph W. Svec III

The Missing Authors Series

Sherlock Holmes and The Adventure of The Grinning Cat
Sherlock Holmes and The Nautilus Adventure
Sherlock Holmes and The Round Table Adventure

"Joseph Svec, III is brilliant in entwining two endearing and enduring classics of literature, blending the factual with the fantastical; the playful with the pensive; and the mischievous with the mysterious. We shall, all of us young and old, benefit with a cup of tea, a tranquil afternoon, and a copy of Sherlock Holmes, The Adventure of the Grinning Cat."
Amador County Holmes Hounds Sherlockian Society

www.mxpublishing.com

Also from MX Publishing

Our bestselling books are our short story collections;

'Lost Stories of Sherlock Holmes' , 'The Outstanding Mysteries of Sherlock Holmes', The Papers of Sherlock Holmes Volume 1 and 2, 'Untold Adventures of Sherlock Holmes' (and the sequel 'Studies in Legacy) and 'Sherlock Holmes in Pursuit', 'The Cotswold Werewolf and Other Stories of Sherlock Holmes' – and many more……

www.mxpublishing.com

Also from MX Publishing

"Phil Growick's, 'The Secret Journal of Dr Watson', is an adventure which takes place in the latter part of Holmes and Watson's lives. They are entrusted by HM Government (although not officially) and the King no less to undertake a rescue mission to save the Romanovs, Russia's Royal family from a grisly end at the hand of the Bolsheviks. There is a wealth of detail in the story but not so much as would detract us from the enjoyment of the story. Espionage, counter-espionage, the ace of spies himself, double-agents, double-crossers...all these flit across the pages in a realistic and exciting way. All the characters are extremely well-drawn and Mr Growick, most importantly, does not falter with a very good ear for Holmesian dialogue indeed. Highly recommended. A five-star effort."
The Baker Street Society

Also from MX Publishing

The American Literati Series

The Final Page of Baker Street
The Baron of Brede Place
Seventeen Minutes To Baker Street

"The really amazing thing about this book is the author's ability to call up the 'essence' of both the Baker Street 'digs' of Holmes and Watson as well as that of the 'mean streets' of Marlowe's Los Angeles. Although none of the action takes place in either place, Holmes and Watson share a sense of camaraderie and self-confidence in facing threats and problems that also pervades many of the later tales in the Canon. Following their conversations and banter is a return to Edwardian England and its certainties and hope for the future. This is definitely the world before The Great War."
Philip K Jones

www.mxpublishing.com

Also from MX Publishing

The Detective and The Woman Series

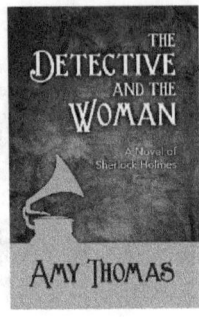  

The Detective and The Woman
The Detective, The Woman and The Winking Tree
The Detective, The Woman and The Silent Hive

"The book is entertaining, puzzling and a lot of fun. I believe the author has hit on the only type of long-term relationship possible for Sherlock Holmes and Irene Adler. The details of the narrative only add force to the romantic defects we expect in both of them and their growth and development are truly marvelous to watch. This is not a love story. Instead, it is a coming-of-age tale starring two of our favorite characters."
Philip K Jones

www.mxpublishing.com

Also from MX Publishing

The Sherlock Holmes and Enoch Hale Series

The Amateur Executioner
The Poisoned Penman
The Egyptian Curse

"The Amateur Executioner: Enoch Hale Meets Sherlock Holmes", the first collaboration between Dan Andriacco and Kieran McMullen, concerns the possibility of a Fenian attack in London. Hale, a native Bostonian, is a reporter for London's Central News Syndicate - where, in 1920, Horace Harker is still a familiar figure, though far from revered. "The Amateur Executioner" takes us into an ambiguous and murky world where right and wrong aren't always distinguishable. I look forward to reading more about Enoch Hale."
Sherlock Holmes Society of London

www.mxpublishing.com

www.ingramcontent.com/pod-product-compliance
Lightning Source LLC
Chambersburg PA
CBHW051513170626
46811CB00002B/802